A tingle of excitement ran along every nerve in her body.

Nice girls like her weren't supposed to have irresistible physical yearnings like this. Nice girls stayed at home, minding the village shop. They didn't dress in midnight-blue velvet and gallivant about in front of foreign aristocracy. Gwen knew her family would be speechless at the mere thought of it. They had made enough fuss when her eldest brother Glyn married a girl from Bristol and moved across the river.

Mrs Williams' sisters had always warned her that Gwen had a wayward streak, and with an unusual surge of devilment Gwen wondered if they might be right…

D0928381

Christina Hollis was born in Somerset, and now lives in the idyllic Wye valley. She was born reading, and her childhood dream was to become a writer. This was realised when she became a successful journalist and lecturer in organic horticulture. Then she gave it all up to become a full-time mother of two and run half an acre of productive country garden.

Writing Mills & Boon® romances is another ambition realised. It fills most of her time, in between complicated rural school runs. The rest of her life is divided among garden and kitchen, either growing fruit and vegetables or cooking with them. Her daughter's cat always closely supervises everything she does around the home, from typing to picking strawberries!

You can learn more about Christina and her writing at www.christinahollis.com

Recent titles by the same author:

THE COUNT OF CASTELFINO
THE TUSCAN TYCOON'S PREGNANT HOUSEKEEPER
THE RUTHLESS ITALIAN'S INEXPERIENCED WIFE
HER RUTHLESS ITALIAN BOSS

THE FRENCH ARISTOCRAT'S BABY

BY
CHRISTINA HOLLIS

First published in Great Britain 2010
Harlequin Mills & Boon Limited,
Eton House, 18-24 Paradise Road, Richmond, Su

ROM
Pbk

© Christina Hollis 2010

ISBN: 978 0 263 87801 1

Harlequin Mills & Boon policy is to use papers that are natural, renewable and recyclable products and made from wood grown in sustainable forests. The logging and manufacturing process conform to the legal environmental regulations of the country of origin.

Printed and bound in Spain
by Litografia Rosés, S.A., Barcelona

THE FRENCH ARISTOCRAT'S BABY

CHAPTER ONE

An awful racket bounced Gwen out of bed before she was fully awake. Stumbling around her bedroom in the afternoon heat, she tried to find her clock. When she did, it was silent. The ringing was coming from somewhere else. It must be her mobile. In horror, Gwen realised she had fallen onto the bed too exhausted to switch on her alarm. She had overslept, and was already at least an hour behind schedule. Now it sounded as if one of her few remaining members of staff was phoning about the evening shift. With growing dread, she searched frantically for her phone. Finally she tracked it down. It was in the pocket of her apron, at the bottom of her washing basket.

'Gwenno! What took you so long to answer the phone, love?'

For once, Gwen was glad her mother rang every day.

'Mam! It's great to hear from you, but this time I *really* can't stop—I've got my hands full, getting ready for this big flash party tonight. I was terrified you were one of the kitchen staff, calling in sick!' She gasped, and then made a face. Blurting out the truth to her mother like that was a big mistake. Everyone back at home had to go on thinking she was making a success of her new life. They *had* to… 'That is—I mean…I've got more than enough people working for me, but each of them has their own speciality. I can't afford to lose a single person!' She finished in a rush, her fingers crossed. In reality, Gwen was desperate to cut costs. Rather than employ enough staff, she was currently doing the work of at least three people. Trying to save money was costing her a lot. She was so exhausted, there had been a real danger she might have dozed off during the party preparations. That was why she had dashed home to snatch a twenty-minute nap in the middle of the day. She checked her watch, and discovered with horror she had been asleep for nearly an hour and a half.

'My God, I should be at the restaurant! We'll never open in time! I've got so much to do!'

Dashing around the room, she tried to gather together her clothes for the evening with one hand, while the other clamped the mobile to her ear.

Gwen's mother had an answer for everything. This disaster was no exception.

'You've told us all about your dozens of staff, Gwenno. Let them start earning all that money you pay them!'

'Dozens of staff? Er…yes, yes, of course I have…it's just that I like to do as much as I can myself. It's my own fault for loving the job so much. I'm still not used to being sole owner of the restaurant, and sometimes it gets a bit much,' Gwen said quickly, the reply sounding horribly false to her own ears. Was that a tinge of suspicion she heard in her mother's voice?

'We didn't lend you all that money to run yourself

into the ground, Gwenno. It was supposed to help you become Le Rossignol's chef-patron.' Mrs Williams said each foreign word carefully. 'See? We're all practising for when we come over to visit you!'

Gwen's heart hit the floor, but she managed to manufacture a careless laugh.

'Great! I can't wait to see you all again. It's been months!'

'It's been four months, three weeks and five days since you finally managed to buy the restaurant,' Mrs Williams said. She sounded almost as proud as Gwen felt, when she had the energy. 'And there was me and your dad worried to death you'd given up a good steady future with us in the shop to chase some silly dream!'

Gwen wanted to cry, but didn't dare. The thought of her family discovering the truth behind her supposedly successful new life in Malotte was more than her pride could stand. She was adamant she could make a success of the business, but times were hard. Every booking had to be treated with great care. Much to Gwen's disgust, that included tonight's reception for a hideous countess. The horrible woman only wanted to make a good impression on her rich stepson. She wasn't interested in Gwen's skill or the restaurant, merely in her own reputation.

Gwen could only hope the man in question would be more appreciative.

Etienne Moreau's day was equally busy, but his timetable ran according to his own schedule. That was exactly as he liked it. Even his social life now ran like clockwork, but he was increasingly finding socialising to be a sick joke these days. People considered his name a big attraction on a charity invitation list, so he sometimes felt obliged to give them what they wanted. *If only I weren't always surrounded by apple-polishers,* he thought, scrubbing long, strong fingers irritably through his thatch of dark hair. A proper conversation wasn't so much to ask, was it? He disliked having to be constantly on the lookout for lame-duck projects, or women on the make.

The country's grandest money men had invited Etienne onto their board of directors. Their idea had been to simply use his title to impress their shareholders, nothing more. Within days they had discovered their mistake. Etienne had been born into privilege, but that had never been enough for him. His late father had considered work undignified, but Etienne had never been satisfied to be simply a name on some headed notepaper.

He sighed. In exactly ninety minutes' time, a servant would be ready to step forward as Etienne descended the main staircase of his chateau. The man would insert a freshly picked carnation into his master's buttonhole before opening the front door. It had been the same in his late father's time, and for as far back as anyone could remember, so Etienne, albeit reluctantly, humoured his faithful staff. In one brief, heart-stopping moment a couple of years ago, he had imagined his own son and heir taking over, in his turn.

But that was before Etienne had learned the truth about a lot of things, including human nature. Now he focused only on his work, and his ruthless single-minded approach had resulted in endless successes. In fact, for a man with nothing to prove, Etienne was proving un-stoppable. A shame that even this was beginning to pall.

I need to find a new challenge, he thought. He had been brought up to slip smoothly into the role of Count of Malotte. Now he was actually in charge, the largely ceremonial role gave him too much time to brood. He wanted distraction. Perhaps this evening's engagement might offer something different?

Gwen showered and dressed in a flash. Unable to face the pile of unopened letters on her dressing table, she stuffed them into a drawer. Lately, they contained nothing but bad news. Her new life was turning out to have some hard, horrible moments, but she was determined not to give up. Opening her wardrobe, she took out the dress she would change into before the guests arrived at Le Rossignol that evening. Gwen's clients at her restaurant expected a total dining experience. That included ex-changing small talk with a calm and assured chef-patron. It was the only part of her job Gwen wasn't keen on, but it was turning out to be a very important source of new business. She had to persevere, and it was tough.

Gwen had always dreamed of becoming the chef in a top-class restaurant. She had managed it in record time by going into partnership with her best friend from catering college. Carys had supplied the glamour and business sense. Gwen had done the cooking, and kept her head down. Their system had worked perfectly, until her partner's romantic adventures had thrown the busi-ness into chaos. Carys had vanished, leaving Gwen high and dry. Unable to find another partner, Gwen had been faced with a stark choice. She could sell up and go home. That would mean admitting to her parents that 'The Le Rossignol affair', as they called it, was a big mistake. Or she could mortgage herself to the hilt and make her new life work, alone. One path led back to the safety of the village shop where she had been born. The other route disappeared into an unknown future, but at least it was her own. She would be independent, without the need to rely on other people.

Gwen had found it no real choice at all. She had spent sleepless nights trying to talk herself out of the mad idea, but in the end her dream had won. Instead of selling up, she had bought the balance of the business. Her family was convinced she was throwing good money after bad. Gwen had a horrible feeling they were right, but would never have admitted that in a million years. Besides, if she managed to pull it off she would have the satisfaction of saying, *I did it all myself.* She had always known it would be hard but now, all alone in a foreign country, there were times when she ached for a shoulder to cry on. One frantically busy day dissolved into another. Time was passing her by so fast. She sighed. Her greatest pleasure came from cooking the food, but she spent more time nowadays pandering to the people who ate it.

Carrying her dress downstairs, she laid it reverently on the back seat of her car. One eye on the time, she hopped into the driving seat and got another nasty shock. When she switched on the ignition, the car's petrol gauge barely moved out of the red zone. She groaned in horror. Not today, of all days! She didn't have time to stop off at the garage. She looked up at the bright cloudless sky, then down the winding country road towards town. It was downhill all the way to Le Rossignol. Maybe it was hot enough for the engine to run on fumes and good luck until she got there.

Five hours later, Gwen poured herself into her stunning dress. It was the only formal gown she had, and it was perfect for an aristocratic party. Cut from midnight-blue velvet, it clung to her generous curves in all the right places. She watched herself in the full-length mirror she had hung in her office to check her appearance at moments like this. Her soft blonde hair coiled like liquid gold over her bare shoulders. The effect was stunning, but Gwen wasn't impressed. All she saw was a girl from the Welsh valleys done up like a dog's dinner in a totally impractical dress that would show every mark.

That was exactly what the snooty countess of Malotte expected to see. With a long-suffering smile, Gwen went out to give her public what they demanded.

The restaurant's bar and lounge area was soon crowded. Girls hired for the evening moved among the glittering guests with trays of tempting titbits. Gwen's eyes darted around the room, looking for her client, the countess. Then her attention was grabbed by something far more interesting. A new arrival stood in the restaurant's entrance. Everything about him made her stop and stare. He surveyed the restaurant's crowded lounge bar with the haughty look of a general inspecting foot soldiers. It was an imposing sight. The newcomer was one of the tallest there, and his austere good looks singled him out in other ways, too. Everyone—absolutely everyone—turned to watch as the mystery man walked in.

To Gwen's astonishment he headed straight for her. Clusters of people standing around in the reception bar parted to let him through.

'*Bonsoir*. You must be Gwyneth Williams.'

He dipped his head in greeting. The fact he knew her name surprised her, and that wasn't all. She could feel him penetrating her polite disguise. His gaze seemed to recognise the social misfit within, and it made her nervous. She disguised her true feelings with a professional smile and stepped forward to greet him.

'*Bonsoir, monsieur.* Yes, I'm chef-patron here. I'm usually shut away in the kitchens, but tonight is a special occasion.'

His dark eyes glittered like jet. 'Indeed. I had no idea how special until a moment ago.' Charm flowed from him as he caught her hand and lifted it to his lips. 'My name is Etienne Moreau. I'm a frequent visitor to this restaurant. I'm sorry we've never met before.'

Gwen was enchanted. Despite the dozens of people surrounding them, he had the ability to make her feel as though they were totally alone. After weeks of work and worry, it felt as though all her Christmases had arrived at once.

'Thank you! Would you care for a drink, Monsieur Moreau?'

One of the waitresses moved forward, but Gwen waved her away. For the first time, socialising was giving her something to enjoy. She swung around to the other side of the bar, glad to have something to do. The sight of a man like Etienne Moreau with his soft dark hair and golden skin was enough to stun anyone into silence. The countess Sophie, who was throwing this reception, had dropped some heavy hints about her stepson's dislike of idle chit-chat. She had warned Gwen to give him a wide berth. If there hadn't been a big balance still outstanding on the party bill, Gwen would have delighted in ignoring the instruction. Now there was only the black marble bar between her and this gorgeous man. It didn't feel like much in the way of protection when Etienne's dark eyes could cut through the crowd like lasers. Gwen swallowed hard, reached for the ice bucket and gripped it tightly. No wonder the countess Sophie was so protective of her stepson. All the women within sight were drooling openly. The object of their desires barely acknowledged them. Gwen tried to behave in an equally offhand manner. She smiled pleasantly at her stellar guest. No one could complain if she was only serving the man. It was her job, after all.

'Excuse me, *monsieur,* what would you like?'

Etienne Moreau had paused to question a nearby guest about a recent business deal. His attention instantly swung back to Gwen. He focused his gaze on her as though she was the very last thing he expected to find at a family party. With warm concentration, his pensive brown eyes took in every detail from her tumble of honey-blonde hair to the curves sculpted by her beautiful blue evening dress. After due deliberation, his inspection returned to her eyes. Then he smiled, and Gwen's world stood still.

'I'd like something you could not possibly offer me over a crowded bar.'

The gentle lilt of his accent should have been relaxing. It had quite the opposite effect on Gwen. The wicked smile lighting his face turned her insides to jelly. She was used to fending off all kinds of trouble from men, but for the first time in her life she felt like meeting it head-on. The sensation made her smile right back at him. Her professional approach might hide the effect he was having on her, but it couldn't steady her voice.

'I—I mean, what would you like to drink, *monsieur*? Le Rossignol has a large selection of fine wines and spirits,' she said, trying to disguise her uncertainty by casually leaning forward against her side of the bar. His dark eyebrows rose in appreciation. Gwen's unspoken reply was to lean back again. He smiled.

'I'll have a *léger Colombien, s'il vous plaît*.'

Coffee was the very last thing Gwen served the sort of people who partied at Le Rossignol, not the first. Despite that, she was ready for anything. At one end of the bar was the best hot drink console she could afford. While she busied herself creating Etienne's coffee, Gwen was aware of him chatting idly with others at the bar, but she didn't hear a word. She was too busy enjoying the sensation of his interest running over her. Although she had her back to him, it was as tangible as a touch. When she turned around, his eyes were warm with possibilities. As she passed him the cup his glance flicked down to her left hand.

'*Merci, mademoiselle.* Won't you have one with me?'

'No, *monsieur*. I'm working.'

His beautiful white teeth flashed in a wicked smile. 'I suppose that means Sophie got to you first. She must have threatened to lay a curse on you, if you distracted me for too long.'

One look and those few words almost made Gwen forget everything she had ever known. Only thoughts of her overdraft stopped her melting into a quivering heap, right there in front of him.

'Not at all, *monsieur*. I'm on duty. To linger with one guest, however charming, would be unprofessional,' she said with an ease that felt anything but natural. 'And now, if you would excuse me, I must circulate.'

The smile Gwen gave him faltered as she saw the warmth in his eyes. Unable to meet the silent laughter dancing there, she left him with as much slow dignity as she could muster.

Etienne sipped his coffee. Darkening with thought, his eyes glittered as he watched her walk away. His companions at the bar were still talking, but he took only a polite interest.

'It didn't take you long to get over Angela, did it, Etienne?' One of the guests laughed, tracking his gaze.

The question brought Etienne back to the present with a jolt. His lip curled with a sneer of disdain. 'Sentiment is for women and children. I don't waste time on it.' Shrugging his shoulder nonchalantly, he pushed the empty coffee cup aside. 'Excuse me. I should go and have a word with the countess Sophie.'

Leaving the bar, Etienne strode away through the reception area without a backward glance. He wished the past could be ignored as easily as he could sideline people. Work sometimes dulled the edge of his pain, but never for long. It was so much easier to skim over the surface of life, moving on to the next sensation before he had too much time to think about it. He spent his days crowding his troubled mind with other people's money worries. When he was able to use his power and influence to help them, it gave him a sense of satisfaction but left his body restless. For hundreds of years the Moreau family had been warriors. Intellectually gifted, Etienne found balance sheets and bank reports easier to read than people—and far more honest. He preferred to use his mind for work and keep his body for more civilised things than warfare.

Right now he was wondering how quickly Miss Gwyneth Williams would surrender to his charm.

As usual, everyone wanted to talk to Etienne. It took him quite a while to track Gwen across the room. A little glance over her shoulder and a half-smile told him she knew he was watching her. That pleased him. It made up for the fact that his stepmother's niece Emilie was in attendance tonight. A plump, pretty girl dressed in a tight sheath of pink satin, she was standing a respectful distance behind the countess. As Sophie Moreau realised Etienne was on his way over, she eased Gwen aside and jostled the astonished Emilie forward. Etienne didn't need to wonder why. He shot a conspiratorial look at Gwen. There was a little crease between her brows as she spoke to the countess, but it disappeared as he caught her eye. Her beautiful face lit up with a mischievous smile, but she was playing hard to get. As he drew closer she disappeared into the kitchens. Etienne was left to corner his stepmother alone.

'Are you having trouble with the staff, Sophie? Would you like me to hunt that woman down and have a word with her?' he offered innocently.

The countess scowled. 'Certainly not. You aren't here to work, Etienne. You're here to tell your cousin Emilie what you think of her. Hasn't she grown?'

There were only two things in Sophie Moreau's favour: Etienne could read her like a book, and she always came straight to the point. Arching one dark eyebrow, he hid his distaste behind a pleasant smile. Lifting the young girl's hand to his lips, he gave it a formal kiss.

'You have, Emilie. How old are you now? It must be all of—sixteen, is it?'

'Eighteen! That's why you've agreed to be guest of honour at her birthday party, next month!' his step-mother hissed.

'I would never let a step-relative down.' Etienne in-clined his head graciously at Emilie. The girl simpered, the restaurant's discreet lighting bouncing off her ortho-dontic scaffolding.

'Emilie will be leaving her boarding school at the end of next term. Unless you can think of a good reason to free her from the dreadful place before then, Etienne?' Sophie leered at him.

Feigning ignorance, Etienne waited.

'Unless…' The countess leaned forward, prompting him. Tiny beads of perspiration were visible on her faint moustache. She stopped squinting and started frowning.

'Oh, for goodness' sake, don't be difficult, Etienne! You need a son and heir to carry on the Moreau family line, and inherit all those beautiful houses of yours!'

Etienne sliced off Sophie's words with a fearsome glare. After a moment's alarm, she surged back with added venom. 'It must be two years since you got your fingers burned by that awful woman—you must think of the future, Etienne.'

'Why? You seem to be doing enough of that for both of us, *step*mother.' Etienne answered with crushing emphasis.

Out in Le Rossignol*'s* kitchens, preparations for dinner were running exactly on time. Everything was ready to go. It all looked immaculate. Gwen had lost count of the compliments her staff and the restaurant had been given as she moved among the guests. Even so, her nerves were in shreds. It didn't help to have the waitresses chattering like magpies with all the gossip they picked up as they circulated with drinks and canapés. As Gwen checked the silver salvers before they were carried out one of the regular waitresses passed on a particularly juicy titbit.

'*Madame* wants to make sure she carries on getting a share of Etienne's fortune after he marries. That's why she's trying to pair him off with her niece.'

'I've told you before, you mustn't pass on anything you hear, Clemence!' Gwen rebuked her, wiping a drop of champagne from one of the glasses. 'It would be horrible for a nice young girl like Emilie to find out people were talking about her.' However, Clemence's words sent evil thoughts flooding into her heart. Secretly, she turned green with envy at the idea.

'Don't worry, Chef, it'll never happen! You only have to read what they say about Etienne Moreau in the papers to know that—'

The doors leading into the restaurant opened, bringing another collection of empty trays for refilling and cutting off Clemence's shameful but undeniably interesting gossip. Beyond the traffic of waiters and waitresses, Gwen glimpsed the countess Sophie and her niece backing away from the impressive count. Clemence saw it too.

'Look—he's given them the brush-off. Now's your chance, Chef! Count Etienne is worth a fortune. He spends a lot in here, and he's our best tipper. Be nice to him!' Clemence said with a wink.

With alarm, Gwen found her heart thumping at the simple mention of his name. She found it hard enough to talk to clients at the best of times. To walk up to this gorgeous man would be impossible for her, unless she had an excuse, and something to hide behind. She found both at the bar. Keen to get opinions on a new Bordeaux she was thinking of putting on the wine list, she poured him a glass. As she carried it over she tried to distract herself from the warm, liquid feeling suffusing her body. It was no good. The magnetism of the count's slumberous dark eyes demanded her full attention. His expression made her forget any worries she might have had about her only formal dress. He liked it, she could tell. The classic cast of his features and the resolute line of his jaw marked him out as something really special. As she drew closer to him Gwen's body responded with an urgency she had never known before. She fought against a tide of desire that threatened to escape in a moan of longing. That scared her. This man was a total stranger, and she was a hard-working, down to earth woman. How could anyone sway her with such strong emotions at first sight? That thought alone was a powerful aphrodisiac.

A tingle of excitement ran along every nerve in her body. Nice girls like her weren't supposed to have irresistible physical yearnings like this. Nice girls stayed at home, minding the village shop. They didn't dress in midnight-blue velvet and gallivant about in front of foreign aristocracy. Gwen knew her family would be speechless at the mere thought of it. They had made enough fuss when her eldest brother Glyn married a girl from Bristol and moved across the river. Mrs Williams' sisters had always warned that Gwen had a wayward streak, and, with an unusual surge of devilment, Gwen wondered if they might be right...

Etienne's day had been totally predictable, but his evening was improving by the minute. He had given his stepmother something to think about, and now he was enjoying the sight of Gwyneth Williams bringing him a second drink. Although he visited Le Rossignol often, he'd never been lucky enough to meet her before. He had heard whispers about her, and they were all true. She really was worth watching. Her voluptuous charms were enhanced by the cut of an evening dress so beautiful, no other woman in the room was worthy of it. Its pacific-blue colouring and glorious texture made him want to reach out, to touch and possess. The sinuous way this woman moved through the crowds towards him made Etienne wish they were the only two people in the place…

He brought himself up short for even considering it. That disastrous liaison with Angela Webbington should have put him off ill-considered flings for life. But who wouldn't be tempted by the charms of a woman like this Gwyneth Williams? It was no wonder the gaze of every man in the place followed her. She had the perfect hour-glass figure—full, soft breasts and a beautifully defined waist emphasising the smooth curve of her derriere. When she reached him and lifted those long dark lashes to reveal the clear beauty of her azure eyes, Etienne re-discovered the full physical meaning of the words 'sexual chemistry'.

'You've been very generous to my staff in the past, *monsieur*. Allow me to offer you this, with the compliments of Le Rossignol.'

Her words lilted like music. They had an immediate effect on Etienne. A powerful chain reaction coursed through his muscular body, coiling in his groin ready for action. She passed him the glass. Their fingers touched for an instant, but before they could exchange any words Gwen was called away. Etienne watched her go, his unwanted drink forgotten. As she passed by a gaggle of male guests one of them said something to her. Etienne was too far away to hear what it was, but saw her round on the man with icy disdain. Roses flared in her otherwise pale cheeks. Etienne instantly began moving forward. Although Gwen looked to be coping, he knew you could never be sure in situations like this.

Gwen counted to ten silently, thinking of the final demand notices she had at home. She had to pander to these awful people. Their word of mouth recommendations were vital if her business was to survive.

'You're wasted in the kitchen!' The groper smirked. 'You look like you're sitting on a fortune, *bonbon*. How about it?'

In one swift movement he stuffed a five-hundred-Euro note into her cleavage.

Gwen's brittle smile was for public consumption only. She pulled out the banknote and dropped it onto the floor.

'I've got plenty more where that came from,' the man scoffed.

'I'm so glad, *monsieur*,' Gwen managed with dignity. Turning her back on the group, she walked back into the safety of her kitchens. Her head was held high. When she looked like that, the staff went quiet.

'Ask Eloise to check the guest list,' she announced into the relative silence. 'She can put a marker on the names of those men sitting beside the aquarium. In future we're going to be fully booked whenever they ring for a reservation. I won't have men who behave like that at Le Rossignol—we don't need them,' she stated, with more conviction than she felt. Right now her business was balanced on such a knife-edge she couldn't afford to turn anyone down. She had to take so much care not to upset her rich clientele. They all knew each other, and word travelled around their clique at the speed of light. The rich stuck together in their own little world. People like her were expected to fetch and carry, and take all the flak. It was so unfair.

It was a relief for Gwen to retreat from the social whirl into the organised chaos backstage. This was the world she knew, and a place where she was in total control. Outside in the restaurant she was expected to be constantly charming and beautiful—something ornamental rather than useful. Here in the noise and movement of the kitchens, she could be herself. She could concentrate on producing the best and most beautiful meals her customers would ever experience. Until that evening, the satisfaction of a job well done had been enough for her. But now something threatened to come between Gwen and her work.

She had been introduced to something—or rather, *someone*—far more potent. Etienne Moreau was already affecting her behaviour. As she'd confronted that drunk she had known the handsome count was watching her. A situation that made her feel like running for the hills had had to be faced in a way she knew would impress him. She needed him to see her in action as the perfect hostess, and totally in control.

Because whenever she glanced in his direction, control was the last thing on her mind.

Etienne saw Gwen's confrontation with her guests, and how she handled it. It was quite obvious Le Rossignol's chef-patron was a woman who knew her own mind. He admired the cool way she managed to defuse the situation herself. *Defuse but not disarm*, he thought, making a mental note to mention the bad behaviour he had seen to some of his more influential friends. He recognised the villains, and they would find themselves excluded from society's more discerning events from here on in. *Not that it's any of my business,* he warned himself, annoyed that the little drama should have unsettled him so much.

For once, when his stepmother begged to parade him in front of a few more of her friends, he was glad of the distraction. While she was busy showing him off, she couldn't return to her favourite subject of what a superb wife and countess her niece would make. That alone would have been a good enough reason to submit to a tour of the gathering, but Etienne had a darker motive. He wanted to keep an eye on the lovely Gwyneth Williams. A natural at moving through polite society, Etienne could appear perfectly charming while his mind was occupied with something else. Tonight, there was only one thing concerning him. Covertly, he watched Gwen as she went about her work. When the rowdy group of men summoned her again he stiffened, noticing a subtle change in her attitude. Her beautiful, heart-shaped face was a carefully managed mask of indifference, but tension was obvious in her rigid bearing and hesitant footsteps. The second she got close enough, one of the group reached out as though ready to paw the smooth curve of her rump. Gwen leapt away with a cry but before she could say anything more Etienne was there, confronting her attacker.

'Leave her alone,' he commanded.

'Says who?' The young man lumbered to his feet. It was obvious he had been drinking before he arrived at the restaurant, and was now well beyond the stage of either good manners or good sense.

'I do.' Etienne's voice was as cold as a blade, and he felt no need to identify himself by the age-old title of

Count of Malotte. Tonight, everyone who was anyone knew who he was.

'Like I care about that!' The drunk swayed, then without warning took a swing at Etienne. Gwen shouted a warning, desperate to save the handsome stranger who had stepped in on her behalf. It was the worst thing she could have done. Distracted by her cry, Etienne was a split second too slow to avoid catching a glancing blow to the side of his jaw.

The party erupted in a flurry. In one smooth movement Etienne seized the drunk and pinioned his arms behind his back.

'Let this be a warning to anyone else with a taste for trouble,' he announced to the crowd as he frogmarched his attacker out of the building. Everyone stared after him. Gwen could not move. If she took one step she knew she would fly straight to the door, desperate to know what was happening. That would make a bad situation worse for her sophisticated guests. Instead, she had to wait along with everyone else. Minutes passed in silence. Then suddenly Etienne was there among them again. Breathing quickly, his dark curls tousled, he acknowledged the spontaneous applause with a diffident smile.

'Your cheek is bleeding,' Gwen said faintly, transfixed by the sight of a thin seam of blood trickling over the otherwise perfect surface of his sun-bronzed skin.

He stopped adjusting his clothes and looked at her.

'There's no need to sound so worried, *mademoiselle*,' he murmured, as though not quite able to believe what she had said.

The strange way he spoke made Gwen think this man

wasn't used to being worried about—not on a personal level, at least. People might bow and scrape before him, but she had a shrewd suspicion they were only out for what they could get, like the countess. A surge of empathy kicked her into action. She knew what it was like to put on a brave show, and she might never get a chance to see such a gorgeous guy at close quarters again.

'Of course there is, *monsieur*. Health and safety would never forgive me for standing by while one of my clients bled all over the place!' she rallied. With a smile, she gestured towards the back of the restaurant. 'Would you mind stepping into my office?'

Her heart was thundering loudly as she spoke. She was amazed he couldn't hear it, and still more amazed at the devastating way he smiled and said, 'Nothing would give me greater pleasure, *mademoiselle*.'

And with that he headed straight for the door marked 'Mlle G Williams—Private.'

CHAPTER TWO

GWEN was busy wondering what she was going to do, now she had persuaded one hundred and eighty pounds of handsome hunk into her office.

The sight of Etienne standing outside on the balcony almost robbed her of the courage to go in. Silhouetted against the setting sun, his broad shoulders and tall, erect frame looked magnificent.

'*Entrez,*' he commanded.

Etienne Moreau was unlike any man Gwen had encountered before, but hearing him speak to her like that came as a shock. Her reply was instant and instinctive. 'I was going to, *monsieur*. It's my name on the door, isn't it?'

He whipped around, as fast as her retort. Gwen didn't have time to be alarmed. Astonishment became amusement as he focused on her face, and laughed.

'Of course. What was I thinking of?' he said with a winning smile.

Gwen had no idea. He was filling her mind with so many disturbing thoughts. It was all she could do to stop her legs trembling as she walked through the room towards him.

'I've retrieved your wine, *monsieur*. And can I thank you for dealing with that drunk? It was so brave. You didn't deserve to get hurt,' Gwen said as she stepped through the French doors and joined him on the balcony.

'Ordinarily I wouldn't have done. He was wearing one of those cameo rings idiot boys have taken to wearing. That's what did the damage.'

As he took the glass of Bordeaux from her the town below exhaled a warm breath into the evening air. It lifted the curtains behind her. Light flooding out from the office illuminated the ragged cut to his cheek. Gwen was transfixed.

'Merci,' he said softly.

'What about that cut?' she managed eventually, her mind whirling with the tiniest details of it. 'I'll fetch the first-aid kit—'

'That won't be necessary.'

The same commanding tone that had summoned her into her own office drew her hand up to his face.

'Oh, but you must at least let me clean it up for you—' Unable to resist, she touched the spot lightly. Her fingers came away dark with blood. With a little gasp of dismay she swayed, accidentally brushing against him. 'I'm sorry, *monsieur*,' she muttered.

Etienne Moreau knew an advantage when he saw one. A smile spread across his face with all the promise of a new day dawning.

'Are you, *mademoiselle?* I'm not. It's brought us together.'

'H-has it?'

Her eyes were wide and very blue, he noticed. It occurred to him that shock must have thrown the sophisticated chef-patron off her stride. The delicate fragrance of roses shimmering around her aroused something primitive in him. There was only one thing to be done. He decided to make everything all right for her, in the way he knew best. After months of growing discontent, this evening was turning into something memorable for him. He glanced at the wine in his hand. The last thing he needed now was alcohol. It might bring him back to earth.

He put the glass down.

A furious tide had engulfed him when he saw that lecherous drunk hassling her. Seeing such a man getting so close to this lovely girl was an outrage. She deserved much better. And now he was alone with her. Desire flamed within his body, fuelled by the purity of her clear blue eyes and those soft, slightly glossed lips. He hungered for her with a raw, naked need that would not and could not be denied.

'Is there anything else you need, *monsieur*?'

Her voice was a whisper, her eyes full of anticipation.

'Yes,' he breathed. 'You.'

She gazed up at him. Her eyes were large and full of questions Etienne could not wait to answer. His body took control, pulling her into his arms and holding her tightly against him. Gwen was in the grip of feelings so powerful that she simply melted against him. His hands went to her hair, his fingers digging through its thick tumble of soft, caramel-coloured curls. Tipping her head back, he feasted his eyes on her face. Uncertainly, she mirrored his movements, raising her hands to the lush darkness of his hair. It was short and silky, tempting her fingers to explore him with the same overpowering need that fuelled his desire. When his beautiful mouth took possession of hers it was with a passion that powered straight through her body.

Gwen had never experienced anything like it. Etienne Moreau overwhelmed her with such fire and urgency that she felt like a leaf in a hurricane. Her heart pounded, while her mind became a perfect storm of images—his tongue penetrating her mouth, his hands luring her onwards until he withdrew, teasing her. Gwen was left quivering from head to foot, at the mercy of so many sensations her brain could hardly cope. Hungry for his kisses, she rose on tiptoe, desperate not to lose contact with his body for an instant. Teased into peaks of excitement, her nipples thrust against the lacy restraint of her bra until it hurt. He was filling her senses so totally she barely noticed. She no longer knew or cared what was right or wrong.

Suddenly the wail of a police siren tore through the streets below, startling them both, and they jerked apart. Once she was deprived of the hard temptation of him, arousal flooded Gwen's brain until speech was almost beyond her.

She looked up at him, still dazed, as he allowed his hands to drop lightly onto her shoulders and gently eased her away from him. Then he stepped back and looked down at her. His lips were slightly parted. She could see from the quick rise and fall of his chest that he was breathing fast. The arms that had held her so tightly now hung loosely by his sides, his hands and their long, strong fingers slightly curved. Her eyes took in every detail of him, from his hawk-like profile and the glint of perfect white teeth against the pale gold of his skin, to his easy stance. Here was a man who took women in his stride. As she slowly returned to earth after their paradise of a kiss a sudden increase in the clatter of silver and china from inside the restaurant dealt the final blow to her dreams. Dinner was being served. She had abandoned her staff when they needed her most. Kissing a man when she should have been supervising them was bad enough. When that man was also a guest and probably a friend of her landlord, her guilt became a real wall of worries.

Gwen had brothers. She knew what men were like. The thought that this aloof man with the smouldering eyes might tell Nick, her landlord, about their kiss made her feel sick. Nick and his family had been good to her, letting her buy out the business for a good price. They had taken a loss on the deal, but it had still cost Gwen everything she'd had and hefty loans from her parents and the bank. Nick was still owner of the little *gite* in the hills where she was staying. His rich, influential friends were Le Rossignol's best customers, so she needed to stay on the right side of them. This was not the way to do it.

A breeze sighed over the balcony, but this time it was chill. It reminded Gwen of the groans of 'I told you so' waiting for her back at home if her dream of running a top-class restaurant in France failed.

Etienne's face was expressionless; he seemed to have

retreated from her. 'This was an accident. Accidents happen,' he said in a low voice.

Gwen tried to catch her breath. It wouldn't be held, and escaped as a sigh. His attitude should have come as a relief to her. Instead it left an aching void. She wanted this man to want her, in exactly the same hot, heady way she wanted him. It nearly sent her over a precipice of temptation. Colour flared in her normally pale cheeks. What had possessed her to do a thing like that? With his relentless masculinity close enough to touch, that was an easy question to answer. Etienne's body was a powerful incentive for Gwen to behave in a way she would never have dreamed possible. He roused her to fever pitch, but now he was leaving behind a burning ache for him, deep within her body.

'Tension expresses itself in many ways,' he added. A tiny muscle flinched in his jaw as he spoke.

The tilt of his chin and that macho dismissal told Gwen all she needed to know. Now she understood why Clemence had warned her about this man. He was the sort who took what he wanted, without offering anything in return. He would never feel the need to feign interest in her as a thinking, feeling human being.

'I discovered long ago that money and manners don't often go together, *monsieur*,' she said icily. 'I'm certainly not proud of this little interlude either, I can assure you.'

Picking up his forgotten glass, she started towards the French doors.

'But I am.' Etienne's voice was low with amusement and he seemed to have recovered his wicked smile, as if the odd tension that had covered him a moment ago had been shrugged away. 'It's in my blood, *cherie*. You are irresistible. I succumbed to your charms. What better reason for pride could there be?' he finished in a throaty whisper.

Gwen gave a huff of disapproval at that, but she was hiding a blush as she hurried away. Those words of his would echo in her head for the rest of her life. *He called me irresistible!* she marvelled. No one had thought to give her such a compliment before. Five feet three with a tumble of unruly honey-blonde waves, she felt too short and shapely to turn heads. Her bright blue eyes with their long dark lashes were a good feature, there was no denying it. *But irresistible? Me?* she wondered, wishing she could believe him. There was no doubt she had preened before her bedroom mirror when she had first tried on this stunning dress, but that had been behind a securely locked door. Now the delectable Etienne Moreau had kissed her, and complimented her. Much more of his talk and she might—just *might*—start believing it!

There was no time for Gwen to try out her budding self-confidence. As she left her office the countess Sophie steamed towards her with an evil glint in her eyes.

'I hope you aren't annoying my stepson,' she warned, a purplish stain flushing through her thick layers of face powder and blusher. 'He doesn't take kindly to being manhandled by the lower orders.'

If only you knew! Gwen thought. The lovely Etienne hadn't been showing any signs of prejudice a few moments earlier.

'I took the count a drink, showed him where the first-aid kit was and thanked him for saving me from unwanted attention. That's all, *madame*,' Gwen said boldly.

The fat, bejewelled countess looked down her fleshy nose at Gwen. 'Good. I hope this sort of thing doesn't happen often. I expect better from a place that charges so much.'

With that, she swept away to the sympathetic company of her grand friends. Gwen felt her eyes filling with furious tears. She pressed her lips together tightly, to stop a vicious retort bursting out. Her bills couldn't be paid until she had banked the balance of this awful woman's invoice. All the loathsome countess had to do in her pampered life was sign cheques and authorise payments. Gwen earned every cent of her money. To get it, she had to smile politely all evening while being bullied and generally treated like dirt by her so-called 'betters'. One of her mother's favourite sayings came back to haunt her: *'The rich get all the pleasure, the poor get all the pain'*.

She bolted into the kitchens. For the rest of the evening she worked behind the scenes, unless it was absolutely vital for her to emerge as the glamorous hostess. She understood cooking and loved it. Socialising was a part of her life she was really beginning to hate.

For the past two years, Etienne had been living under a heavy cloud of memories. His relentless lifestyle of work and partying was a reaction to it. He had been dead to pleasure for so long, something as simple as that reckless moment with Gwen should never have been able to lighten his mood. Yet somehow it had. There was something about her so unlike the others; it made him smile to think about it. He knew he should be wary, but it was difficult to forget the girl's proud assurance that she wouldn't be boasting of the experience. Etienne had been burned by kiss-and-tell merchants in the past. He knew the way they worked. That, and the fact she kept to her kitchen for most of the rest of the evening, made this little *mademoiselle very* unusual. As he circulated and made polite noises to his friends and acquaintances Etienne kept half an eye on the kitchen doors. Whenever she came out, she would scan the party, but when she made eye contact with him she always blushed and looked away. He wasn't about to put her on the spot by approaching her again. That would only encourage Sophie to get up on her hind legs. He was content to appreciate the divine Mademoiselle Williams from a distance. Her rare appearances made an otherwise dull evening worthwhile. To his surprise he found himself totally unable to take his eyes off her.

It was a long time since any woman had done *that*.

Eventually, the happy racket out in the restaurant died down. Chauffeured limousines queued up outside to collect their glamorous owners. Gwen pasted on her sociable smile, and went out to wish each and every one of them a good night. She looked forward to gazing up at Etienne one last time, but she was to be disappointed. The whisper around the kitchens was that he had left earlier with a few friends. Gwen was quick to stop her staff gossiping, but that didn't prevent her listening to what they said. Apparently the more restless spirits had gone on to an exclusive casino in town.

A long time later, Gwen said goodbye to the last of her staff. Then she locked the door with a thankful sigh. As usual, she was the last to leave. Checking that everything was spotless after the party and ready for the next opening took a long time. With no money to pay more than a skeleton staff, Gwen always tried to make life as easy as possible for them all. Once she was sure the whole place was perfect, she checked again. Her upbringing had convinced her that you couldn't be too careful when profits were being squeezed like a ripe Jaffa orange. Work absorbed so much of her time that her high standards were allowed to slip a bit once she locked the restaurant door behind her. There was never enough energy left after work for perfection in her everyday life. It didn't usually matter, but tonight it was destined to come back and haunt her.

The downward spiral began when she put the key into the ignition of her little car. The engine had to be coaxed into life, and the reason was easy to remember from earlier that afternoon. The petrol gauge was now well into the danger zone. Gwen dropped her head onto the steering wheel and groaned. She had meant to pop out before the garage closed and fill up, but there hadn't been time. Now it was far too late to try. She wondered briefly about going back into her office and trying to sleep on the floor. Her nice comfy bed called too loudly, so she abandoned that idea. All she wanted to do was get home. She pointed her tiny Citroen in the right direction and hoped for the best.

It was a bad idea. The car spluttered to a halt halfway up the twisting mountain road leading to her rented cottage. With a sigh, she nosed it up onto the verge. Unlocking its boot, she grabbed the petrol can. There was barely an eggcup full of fuel inside it. A couple of weeks earlier she had given the contents to one of the waiters to top up his moped. She had totally forgotten to refill the can.

Gwen was faced with a long, dark walk home. Locking the Citroen, she started off. With no one to blame for the situation but herself, she tried to make the best of it. During the day, the views from this road over the Mediterranean were spectacular. At night the uphill journey was breath-robbing rather than breath-taking, although there were compensations. A million stars speckled the sky from one horizon to the other. If that wasn't enough to take Gwen's mind off her blistered toes, the nightingales that gave her restaurant its name were in full song. It was the perfect opportunity to let her mind wander back to that breathtaking kiss with the man who had called her irresistible.

Her head was so full of romance she was only dimly aware of a wholly man-made sound attacking the peace and quiet of the hillside. It took the blazing spotlights of a fast car to bring her to her senses. She jumped off the road in panic, but the vehicle slowed dramatically. Drawing level with her, it paused. The driver opened his door and hailed her.

'Ah, *c'est le chef anglais*! Where are you going on such a dark and lonely night?'

It was him. Etienne Moreau. Gwen was hardly able to believe it. He was behind the wheel of a sleek, low, sports car and with relief she saw he was alone. To have met the gorgeous Etienne with another woman so soon after that wonderful kiss would have been unbearable.

'I'm on my way home. My car broke down.' Gwen smiled ruefully, hoping he wouldn't want details. This was the man who called her irresistible. She didn't want her fantasy wrecked by hearing him call her an airhead for running out of petrol.

'The red Citroen C1 with the parking scrapes and missing offside wing mirror, parked half a kilometre back?'

Gwen nodded, trying not to look pained. That was all she needed. A fantasy man so perfect he knew enough about cars to recognise an idiot when he saw one.

'Get in. I'll give you a lift.'

Gwen looked over his impressive car as it purred contentedly beside her. And then the look in his eyes. They mirrored his words, after that brief moment of passion… *You are irresistible…*

Panic overwhelmed her. It was one thing to fantasise about a man. With her dream threatening to come true, she felt totally inadequate.

'N-no—it's OK. I'm fine. Totally. I'm nearly home. I couldn't possibly…'

The wider he smiled, the faster her voice dwindled.

'Nonsense. Get in. How could I let you walk any further on those stilettos, and still call myself a gentleman?' he added with perfect logic, casting an appreciative glance at Gwen's small, shapely feet. They were peeping out from beneath the hem of her dress as she held it up, away from the long grasses of the verge. She let her hands fall, freeing the folds of material to hide her painfully impractical shoes.

'So—will you accept a lift from me now?'

Gwen sighed. Her feet did hurt, the road was long and dark and Etienne's warm car, not to mention the man himself, looked wonderfully appealing.

'Thank you. That's very kind.' It was tricky keeping the apprehension out of her voice.

Without a word, Etienne took the magnum of champagne that was propped up on the passenger seat. 'You'll be a much more interesting companion than this, *ma chef anglais*. I won it in a charity auction! Perhaps I will donate it as a prize somewhere else.' He laughed as he got out of the car and walked around to where Gwen stood. Filling her arms with the heavy foil-wrapped bottle, he opened the car door for her. Gwen thanked him with a smile.

Getting into the confined space of the passenger seat was another trial. It sharpened her nerves to the point where she had to say something to cover her embarrassment. 'Although I should tell you, *monsieur*, I'm Welsh, not English.'

'Ah, that explains it,' Etienne nodded sagely, slipping into the driver's seat beside her. He paused, one hand on top of the steering wheel.

'Before we start, give me your keys. I'll arrange for someone to collect your car, and get it fixed.'

'Thank you, that's really kind,' Gwen muttered, glad he would never see the tell-tale bill. When she was safely belted in, he pushed his sports car into gear and powered on up the hill.

She watched him, her eyes narrowed.

'Why should the fact that I'm Welsh explain anything, Count?'

Etienne gave her a lazily superior smile. 'That rebellious streak of yours…the way you chose to try and walk home in those ridiculous little shoes instead of phoning someone for help… I should have guessed. And don't bother using my title,' he added casually. 'In my experience, people who call me by it are only looking to gain some advantage.'

Gwen felt slightly affronted, having never tried to gain anything from anyone in her life. 'OK, Monsieur Moreau.'

'It's Etienne.' His voice crackled, then softened as he asked, 'Where do you live?'

'I'm staying in Nick's *gite*, right at the top of the hill. You can drop me anywhere that's convenient for you.'

'And you are his fiancée's best friend, Gwyneth.' Etienne's accent turned her name into something beautiful and exotic, but his words were an accusation.

Gwen stiffened. No matter how gorgeous he was, she couldn't stop herself reacting angrily.

'I was his *ex*-fiancée's *ex*-best friend. And, please call me Gwen!'

'*Dommage!*' He inhaled sharply. 'That's some reaction. What caused the split between you?'

Gwen wondered where to start. She felt like blaming Carys for all her problems, but that wasn't entirely fair. Nobody had held a gun to Gwen's head and made her buy out Nick and Carys' share of the business. 'Well, she upset Nick *and* eighteen months' worth of arrangements by running off with another man on the very day of their wedding. She's cost me a fortune by abandoning our partnership, and I'm so shattered I hardly know what day it is any more.'

She hadn't meant to sound so resentful, but it was impossible not to warm to her theme. Etienne glanced at her. Despite the darkness, he was clearly shocked.

'What happened to the unbreakable bonds of sisterhood? All for one, one for all, and take the man for everything he's got?'

'I'm old-fashioned,' Gwen said primly. 'I expected our business partnership to be like marriage—forever. And an engagement is almost as binding—certainly when it gets all the way to the big day.'

'Are you saying you would rather see your best friend trapped in marriage to a worthy, predictable man like Nick, rather than let her follow her heart?'

'I'd rather things were exactly as they were, with Carys still my partner. She knew what Nick was like before she agreed to marry him. Why did she have to take off like that, all of a sudden? She left me right in the lurch,' Gwen grumbled, heaving another huge sigh. 'I thought she was resigned to life with Nick. I'd always told her not to expect carnivals when he was in town, but she wouldn't listen!'

'That isn't what I told Nick when he asked me to be his best man,' Etienne growled. He was staring straight ahead at the road and gripped the steering wheel with both hands for once.

Gwen was amazed. 'I never saw you at the supposed wedding?' she ventured.

That day, she had hardly seen anyone beyond her crew of catering staff. She had been determined to put on the perfect reception as well as acting as bridesmaid, but one thing was certain. However busy, she could never have missed seeing Etienne. He would have stood head and shoulders over the rest of the guests in every meaning of the phrase.

'Like Carys, I cancelled at the last moment. My father's funeral was held on the same day.'

'Then I'm sorry,' Gwen said quietly.

Etienne made a small gesture of acceptance, but added, 'Thank you, but my father the late count was nearly ninety. He died peacefully, in his sleep.'

'All the same, it must have been a horrible experience for you.' Gwen fell silent. For once, she was wishing her own family weren't so far away.

'And?' He prompted, when she had been lost in thought for some time.

Puzzled by the questioning note in his voice, she looked at him. He pierced the shadowy interior of the car with a sly grin. In reply she frowned and shook her head in a silent appeal for more details.

'This is where you ask me what he left.'

'Do I? Why?' Genuinely confused, Gwen picked up her handbag as Etienne turned his car into the narrow driveway leading to her home.

'Because that's what single women always do when they meet me.'

Gwen paused as the cold, hard meaning of his words sank in. They were weighed down by the resignation in his voice. Here was a man who had everything—looks, style, a title, the money to back it all up—and no doubt all the hangers-on that came with such privileges.

'Oh, dear. You're almost making me feel sorry for you a second time!' She chuckled self-consciously. 'And there was me about to invite you in for coffee, to thank you for running me home. I'll bet your fan club all do *that,* too!' She tried to laugh off the confession. To her surprise, he joined in.

'Yes. Until tonight, I've always refused—but for one night only, I might allow myself to be tempted by a chef-prepared *café noisette*—and perhaps a little something to go with it?' he added in a wicked whisper.

The intimacy in his voice stroked a finger of desire all the way down Gwen's spine. Accepting a lift from a strange man was right out of character for her. Inviting him into her home was something else again.

It must be the season for taking risks.

She drew in a long, slow breath. The sophisticated tang of his aftershave bolstered her courage until she was able to speak with hardly a tremble in her voice.

'If you're sure an invitation wouldn't be too pre-dictable?'

'You're doing the inviting. It's your call, Gwen.'

Her mouth went dry. He was putting her in the driving seat, but she had never felt so close to losing control. When she spoke, she could only manage a faint whisper.

'I wanted to thank you for saving me tonight, not only from that…' she had to choose her words carefully, in case the drunk was one of Etienne's friends or rela-tives '…guest, but from a long walk home, as well. That's two rescue missions in one evening. It seems only fair to offer you coffee.'

'Then the least I can do is to accept.' He smiled, and the starlight seemed to dance in his eyes. Gwen was overwhelmed. It took a lot of concentration to get out of the car, find her house key and open the door. She was trembling with sheer amazement at what was happening. Etienne Moreau could stop her heart simply by looking at her. She had thought she would never see him again after the party—but here he was, coming into her house to drink coffee!

She groped for the light switch and pressed. Nothing happened. Etienne was following her closely. Although the thought of him so close behind her was wickedly tempting, she kept moving. The bulb in the hall must have blown, and she had to reach the wall lights before either of them stumbled in the dark. She clicked the second set of switches. There was still nothing. A little breeze followed them into the house and sent a sheet of paper flickering off the telephone table. Gwen clapped a hand to her face in horror as she remembered what it was. The electricity bill. How long had she been promising herself she would get around to paying it? Too long, as far as the electricity company was concerned.

Etienne bent down and picked it up.

'Is this important?' It was too dark for him to read inside the house, so he stepped back outside. Gwen darted after him, but she was too slow.

Glancing at the bill, he made sympathetic noises. 'So this means we'll be drinking chilled champagne rather than hot coffee!' He shrugged. 'I can live with that.'

'No—I'm sorry, I can't possibly invite you in when I've got no power!' Gwen peered around helplessly in the gloom for inspiration. 'But if you were desperate for a drink, I could light a fire in the old range and boil a pan of water on that—'

She stumbled to a halt in the face of his devastating smile. This had been the perfect chance to spend a little while longer basking in it. She had blown it. He wouldn't want to sit in a dark house. Every second in his company was worth losing a whole night's sleep, but it was slipping away through her fingers. Gwen cursed herself silently.

'I'm such a fool—first the car, and now this!' she announced, already moving towards the front door again. 'I'm so sorry I can't offer you anything, Etienne.'

She was getting ready to close the door behind him when he left, but he stayed where he was.

'Let me be the judge of that, Gwen. Why don't we talk about it over champagne at my place instead?'

His voice was as soft as a breeze moving through the pine trees outside.

Gwen had been busily covering her disappointment by fussing with the door. At his words she stopped. Maybe there was a God in heaven after all! She was getting a second chance. For a heartbeat she allowed herself to experience the fierce thrill of anticipation. Then reality supplied a quick cold shower.

'You don't know how much I'd really love to, Etienne, but I shouldn't…'

'I know,' he crooned, his voice warm with understanding. 'So let's go.'

Reaching out, he caught hold of her hand. His palm was as smooth and warm as his seduction technique.

Gwen's body tried to follow him, but her mind was weighed down with responsibilities.

'Oh, Etienne, I *can't*…maybe we should just say goodnight and leave it at that…' She managed to hang back, but disappointment trailed from her every word. 'I'm so sorry, but I need to be up early. It's another really busy day tomorrow and I have to be on top form…'

He let go of her hand. Looking down, he directed his expression of burning intensity straight into her soul. But when he spoke, his words were directed more to himself.

'I've stumbled on a woman who would put an early night before coffee with me?' he said slowly.

He seemed taken aback, musing over what had obviously never happened before. Gwen smiled.

'Believe me, Etienne, it's a tough call. But don't worry. Your reputation as a ladies' man is completely intact. Nothing would have persuaded me to miss out on coffee with you—apart from a seven a.m. delivery to Le Rossignol.'

His roguish smile completely overwhelmed her, and he took her hand a second time. 'I'll have someone deal with the delivery. After all, you must admit that coffee and conversation would round off the evening perfectly?' Leaning forward, he whispered softly in her ear. 'Very few people refuse me.'

His dark eyes were teasing her and his beautiful mouth tempted her even more than his words. He was good—*very* good. Gwen felt herself waver. Would it be so bad? Just for one night—to be a little irresponsible?

Her hesitation was all it took to make Etienne smile again and Gwen melted. She forgot all her money worries—some things were beyond price and she gave a slow nod of assent.

Releasing her hand, Etienne flipped the car keys out of his pocket and began to walk away from the house. When Gwen didn't follow him instantly, he stopped and faced her.

Watching him warily, Gwen ran her hand up and down the edge of the door. He raised a mocking brow.

'What's the hold-up? Why are you looking at me like that?'

She moved uncomfortably inside her seductively sleek velvet dress.

'I'm still not quite sure…this is all so sudden…'

'Shh!' Laughing, Etienne put a finger to his lips. Then he reached out and caught her by the hand again. 'You talk too much, Gwen. Don't build obstacles where there aren't any. Merely accept what I'm offering.'

Oh, if only…she thought.

CHAPTER THREE

WITHIN seconds, Gwen locked up and bounced into the passenger seat of his car. She was breathing fast, and he noticed.

'Do I make you nervous, Gwen?' His smile flashed very white in the darkness as he nosed his car along the narrow drive. When they reached the lane he turned back down the hill.

Gwen put a hand to her chest. She could feel her heart fluttering like a butterfly in a box.

'No! Well—a little—it's just that I'm not in the habit of going back to the house of someone I've only just met. We've only really exchanged a few words.'

'I seem to remember we exchanged a *little* more than words,' Etienne said, his beautiful French accent giving the words a cadence that spoke straight to the soft, malleable centre of her being.

Gwen looked away, blushing furiously. He was waiting for her to respond, she could tell. His presence was so overwhelming she felt his gaze linger over her like a caress. Then, just as noticeably, its power flicked away from her as he turned his car in at a pair of huge, wrought-iron gates. As Gwen looked up at them her eyes widened.

'My goodness!'

He was unimpressed by her reaction. 'You have never seen these gates before?'

'It's not that. I pass them every day on my way to and from work. I just never dreamed I'd actually get to see who lives here, or what's on the other side of them. That's all.' She gazed around, wondering what on earth she was letting herself in for.

'Not many people do,' Etienne said firmly as a security guard let his car pass. 'Everyone needs a place where they can get away from the glare of publicity. Somewhere they can be themselves. This chateau is mine. It's not my ancestral home—that's on the Loire, *naturellement.*'

There was a long, wide approach road to his hillside home. The chateau looked like a fairy castle cut from black velvet and pinned against the star-speckled sky.

'It's beautiful,' Gwen breathed as Etienne brought his sports car to a halt in front of the South front.

'Wait until you see it in daylight.'

The car's interior light flared as he opened his door. Gwen glimpsed something close to a smile on his face. It had vanished by the time he opened the passenger door to let her out. With one hand he relieved her of the huge champagne bottle. As she stood up his other hand hovered so close to her body she tensed with the expectancy of his touch. When it came, he brushed his palm lightly against the small of her back. The sensation made her gasp, but he intended only to guide her towards his house. His touch fell away at the sound. When they reached the front door he stood aside to let her enter the grand, marble hall first.

'I'll swap this for a more convenient size.' He indicated the bottle in his hand, its foil glittering like gold beneath the security lights. 'Make yourself at home, Gwen. I keep very irregular hours, so my staff do not wait up for me,' he said as she looked up in awe of the large, high-ceilinged room lined with family portraits. Then he disappeared into his warren of a house.

Gwen gazed at the splendour, wondering how anyone could call a lofty old place like this home. It glittered with more gilt and antiques than a museum. The wide open spaces of it made her feel small and uncomfortable. Uneasy at Etienne's absence, she lowered herself onto the very edge of a chair set beside the doorway. She wanted to know what he was doing while he was out of sight. The urge to go and look for him only faded when she heard his sure, steady footsteps again. They were growing closer at a leisurely pace. She tensed, wary of his return but at the same time desperate to see him again.

He didn't disappoint her. As he strolled into the room she fancied he was taller, darker and more imposing than she remembered. She took in every detail of his strong profile and smooth, flawless brow. He accepted her scrutiny with a smile that made her blush.

'Supper has been laid out in the summer drawing room. Join me. We will have champagne later.'

'Are you sure there is enough for two?' Even as she spoke Gwen knew it was a silly question.

'My kitchens always provide plenty,' he said amiably.

'Well…if you're sure they won't mind…'

In the low light, his eyes became intense dark pools. 'You shouldn't worry too much about what other people may think or say, Gwen. This is your life, to live as you want.' He levelled a gaze at her that flickered with intent. Gwen wished she had that sort of courage. From the moment she'd first spotted Etienne entering the party, her head had been filled with thoughts of him. His presence had drawn her attention time and time again. The first time they'd been alone together, she had been powerless to resist his attraction. Now she looked up at him in the certain knowledge he could easily rob her of her last strands of self-control. He was on his home ground, the ideal place to prove how strong his hold over her was.

'I can't do this,' she said faintly. This was unknown territory for Gwen. Her fingers went to the watch strap she always fiddled with when she was nervous.

'I've arranged for your restaurant delivery to be dealt with. You've got absolutely nothing to worry about. It's not that late,' he intoned gently.

'Not for you, maybe, but…I'm beginning to think this is another mistake, Etienne. I should never have come here. I should go…' She sprang to her feet, desperately trying to prove to them both that she was still her own woman. It was hopeless.

'No, you shouldn't. Do you *honestly* think I would let you go back to a house with no power or light?' Etienne's voice was reassuringly hypnotic. 'I can't let you suffer in darkness. Stay here, Gwen. Nothing will happen that you do not want to happen.'

When he said it like that, there was no question of

her going anywhere else. They both knew why she was really here. The only connection it had with electricity was the sizzle of arousal whenever she looked at him.

After all, Gwen thought defiantly, she had been working flat out for months. She was long overdue some pleasure. And she was here in France to live out her dreams—surely that allowed for a little adventure as well? Looking up into Etienne's heart-stopping expression, she knew there would never be a better time to indulge herself.

The second she softened, Etienne moved forward and held out his hand for her. She tentatively placed her palm in his, in a gesture of trust, and he led her through the cool, echoing shadows of his chateau to a small, intimate dining area. Delectable-looking food was laid out on a table along one side of the room. He walked past it, and poured them both a shot of strong coffee. Gwen looked at its colour uncertainly.

'That looks so strong. I'll never sleep tonight,' she murmured.

A leonine smile widened Etienne's generous mouth.

'Good.'

His voice was as silken as the touch he laid on her arm. It slid over the thin fabric of her light jacket until it reached her shoulder. Gwen was transfixed. Her eyes were fastened to his every movement. Then she made the fatal mistake of transferring her attention to his eyes. From that moment on she was totally lost. She had spent her whole life playing by the rules. Now she was staring rebellion straight in the face, and it was wonderful.

'I—I don't know what to do, Etienne.'

'Stay with me tonight.' His voice was husky. 'I haven't felt like this in a long time. Far too long.'

Gwen's mouth went dry. Etienne Moreau must be a very lucky man. She had never felt as good as this in her entire life. A tiny voice whispered warnings in her ear, but it was drowned out by her thundering pulse. The man of her dreams was already moving on from entrancing her mind to working his magic on her body. He took her in his arms, and a sultry heat warmed a secret place between her thighs. It sent waves of desire rolling through her body. She felt her nipples peak as his irises expanded with desire for her. When he bent to plunder another kiss from her lips, Gwen was quick to respond. She mirrored his demands in a way that made him purr with pleasure.

She clutched at him. The unexpected strength of her physical reaction was almost frightening. She felt his hands slip inside her jacket, easing it off her shoulders. He held her tightly, her breasts compressed against the hard masculine plane of his chest. Her body craved more of this new experience. This felt so wild and free, oo right. It was such a wonderful release from work and worry. She surrendered herself to pleasure. Her lips parted, eagerly enjoying the expert touch of his. In response he slid his hands over her inviting, velvet-clad body and held her close to him.

'Do you still want that coffee?' He chuckled softly into her hair.

Gwen shook her head. 'I want to go on doing this.' Her breathy whisper escaped into the night. She raised her hands to ruffle eager fingers through the midnight darkness of his hair. Her responses felt so natural, so good, she couldn't have stopped if she'd wanted to.

His kisses sought out all the delicate places on her throat, turning Gwen weak with longing. The more she responded to his touch, the more obvious his need for her became.

'I want you. Stay here with me tonight,' he repeated, nuzzling into her neck.

Despite the delicious lassitude flooding her body, Gwen retained enough sense to realise this was a turning point. She had been careful and sensible all her life. There had been boyfriends, but she had never been tempted like this before. Etienne's touch stroked away all her preoccupation with study and work. The idea of pushing him away made her ache with unfulfilled longing. She wanted him, whatever that meant. The alternative was to leave right now and never look back. Gwen knew she could not do that. The memory of what might have been would surely haunt her for ever. It was impossible to believe that any other man could ever make her feel like this. To turn her back on Etienne would condemn her to a lifetime of wondering.

'But I'm nothing to you…' Gwen knew that was how it worked. She slaved to put on glittering parties; Etienne moved through them like a comet in the night sky.

He silenced her with another incredible kiss. 'Tonight we are everything to one another. Let tomorrow take care of itself,' he murmured, searing her with the raw heat of passion.

Then his smile reached right down into the depths of her soul and rocked it to its foundations.

He wants me, she thought in wonder. Suddenly, that

made him the most important thing in her life. Right now she was the centre of his universe. That thought alone was enough to make her stretch out and experience life. She had spent months sacrificing everything. This was surely a moment to indulge herself for once.

'Yes…' she murmured.

Her reply unleashed the full power of his kisses. As he held her against his body she felt the ridge of his erection, pressing proud and hard against her. It was tangible proof that he needed her, and acted on Gwen like the finest aphrodisiac.

He carried her up wide stone stairs and through hallways sketched in moonlight. When they reached a room warm with the fragrance of cedar wood he closed the door behind him and laid her down on a wide, soft bed scattered with pillows and cushions. Not sure what she should do or say, Gwen raised herself on her elbows. His magnificent silhouette hovered over her, and she was unable to take her eyes off it. He bent down and began kissing her again with an urgency that made her dizzy.

'I've been looking forward to this all evening,' he murmured.

Gwen's breasts strained within the tightly boned bodice of her evening dress. Excitement defined the peaks of her nipples through its sumptuous fabric. Etienne's hands were drawn to explore her. He brushed the thick mane of her luxuriant hair back over her shoulders so that his touch could run unhindered over her sensuous curves. He took his time, relishing the narrowness of her waist and the full, tempting flare of her hips.

'Your body is so beautiful, *chérie.*'

'Really?' Gwen was so astonished she could hardly speak.

He nodded. 'You are exactly what I need. The moment our eyes met I knew you would breathe life into my existence.'

His voice was as soft as a summer breeze across the maquis. The warmth of his words sent a shiver of anticipation along her spine. In her innocence she reached for him, looking for reassurance. As her hands met at the back of his neck the silkiness of his hair and the smooth warmth of his skin inspired her. She could not stop exploring him, moving her touch over his skin and hair and clothes. Catching the end of his formal black tie, she was surprised at how easily it came undone, slithering free from the collar of his shirt.

His perfect white teeth flashed a smile. His eyes were dark pools of temptation, waiting to engulf her.

'I hope I'm not being too reckless,' she breathed.

Shrugging off his jacket, he lay down beside her, kissing and caressing her with a skill that made all rational thought slip away. Whenever Gwen tried to think beyond the moment, his fingertips brushed off her thoughts. They ran over her with such skill that the future became something that happened to other people, not to her. She was suspended in wonder. Etienne wanted her, so nothing should be allowed to stop him.

Her pulse sang to the rhythm of his body as it moved against hers. In one slow, smooth movement he unzipped her beautiful velvet dress all the way down the back. Then he peeled away its dark blue velvet, revealing her pale, pure body within. Gwen felt a tingle of apprehension. Etienne didn't notice her slight hesitation. He was totally absorbed by the sight of her full breasts, beautifully contoured by the white lace of her bra. Lowering his head, he kissed the darkness of each nipple through its crisp white covering. A cascade of new sensations rippled through Gwen, escaping in a moan of pleasure. A light dew of excitement bloomed over her entire body. She warmed beneath his hands, but he pulled away from her. An ache of longing low down in her belly twisted like a knife. She reached out to stop him leaving her. Then she realised he had only let her go so he could strip off his own clothes.

His body was a revelation to her, but she felt a first frisson of fear. The phrase 'an innocent abroad' rose up to taunt her. What would an experienced man like Etienne make of her? Then he moved in close to her again and the need to reach out and touch him drove every other thought from her mind.

He was built like an athlete. The taut muscles of his broad chest and sleek long limbs rippled. Lit by pale light from his bedroom windows, they gleamed like liquid gold beneath his smooth skin.

'I'm all yours,' he said thickly.

Her hands slid over the smooth glory of his pectorals until they reached the crisp dark curls of his chest hair. Tracing the narrow band of it down until it widened across his belly, her fingers hesitated, and then reached for his proud manhood. At the brush of her fingers he let out a long moan of pleasure. With that encouragement, Gwen couldn't resist going further.

Encircling him, she felt skin as delicate as an eyelid slide beneath her touch.

'Slowly, *chérie*! You go too fast!' His laughter was soft and low in the dusky light. Pulling her up into his embrace, he kissed her again, long and hard as he freed her from the restriction of her bra. As it fell away he moved his attention from her mouth to her breasts. Rolling her onto her back, he teased one nipple with the tip of his tongue while rolling the other between the pads of his thumb and forefinger. Gwen was seized by a fever of excitement. It tossed her around on the bed until she was nearly senseless. When his hand slipped down to explore the curve of her bottom, she arched her back, thrusting against his touch. In response his fingers slipped beneath the flimsy fabric of her panties, pulling them away in his eagerness to explore the warm secrets of her femininity. She shuddered with pleasure as his fingertips found her little bud and teased it into life. Her breath came in staccato sobs, the foreign language of sensual delight. She writhed beneath his touch, the sheer cascades of pleasure almost too much to bear.

'Watching you is the most erotic thing I have ever seen,' he whispered, gathering her up in his arms and covering her with his body. As he slid between her thighs Gwen sobbed with a purely sexual need that could no longer be denied.

Etienne looked down at the beautiful creature lying beneath him on his bed. This was a moment to be savoured. He had never in his life experienced desire like this. Gwen had brought him to such a peak, his entire being sang with it. Gazing at her fragile beauty, he saw his red-hot desire reflected in her eyes. As he plunged into her warm welcoming body she cried out, clutching at him as he filled her with one ravishing, potent thrust.

'Did I hurt you?' He gasped, looking down at her.

'No—I'm all right,' Gwen exclaimed. The pain was already a memory as her body moulded to his in growing excitement. She felt as though she were born to be one with him, and it was unbelievably good. 'Please…don't stop…' she implored.

Etienne's gaze cleared. Her voice and smile were urging him on, and yet her body had resisted.

'Are you a virgin?'

'I was,' she murmured, struggling to open her eyes in the face of another rising tide of passion.

'Why didn't you tell me, *mon amour*?'

Gwen tried to think, but his body was too much of a distraction. 'I thought it would stop you wanting me,' she said eventually.

He shook his head. 'I should have been the judge of that, *ma chérie*.' Then he placed a single reverent kiss on her lips.

When he moved his hips again she felt the whole hot, hard insistence of him willing her to respond. She reacted to his proud dominance instantly, an unquenchable fire running all over her body. She cried out, not in pain, but for release from a desperate search for satisfaction. At last he slid his hands into the small of her back and pulled her tight against his body, catapulting her to orgasm. She flew among the stars as time stood still. Her body gripped him in spasms of exquisite pleasure, drawing him on to the point of no return. With a guttural cry he shuddered to a climax and she was there, her body one with his.

Gwen relaxed into his embrace with a sigh of absolute contentment. She had never felt so close to any other human being in her entire life. Etienne had coaxed her body to heights she had never imagined. A delicious lassitude washed over her, until a dark cloud crept over her horizon. She would have liked nothing better than to talk with him now, but found she couldn't. His rejection when they had kissed in the office dragged her back to earth like a lead weight. If she tried to build on this heaven by breaking the comfortable silence that lay between them now, he might be struck by second thoughts this time, too. What if he came to his senses and dumped her?

'I must go,' she mumbled, determined to jump before he could push her. Quicker than summer lightning Etienne's arm snaked out. His hand closed around her arm, preventing her escape.

'Stay,' he murmured in an echo of his command to her earlier that night.

Pulling her back against his body, Etienne buried his face in her soft, flower-scented hair. He smiled to himself as he drifted between waking and sleeping. This woman really was one of a kind. She was the first who had ever volunteered to leave his bed. He normally had trouble in evicting one-night stands. He was a proud man, and was mildly surprised to find he hadn't taken Gwen's escape bid as a snub. Instead he found it refreshing—especially as she snuggled back into the curve of his body with an ease that felt totally natural.

A girl like Gwen Williams was exactly what he needed. His stepmother was always trying to marry him off. What would *her* reaction be if she heard about this? His mouth twitched in a smile. Gwen certainly wasn't countess material, but that didn't matter to Etienne. Although bitter experience had put him off marriage for life, he was an honourable man. And what red-blooded male could resist taking a mistress as gorgeous as Gwen? It was an opportunity made in heaven. This was the first time in years he had felt free to give his powerful libido its head. Gwen was sex appeal and innocence in one irresistible combination. She was the perfect antidote to his working life, his grasping stepmother and her hoard of needy relatives. Gwen was as willing and eager to please him as he was to indulge her.

The thing that most appealed to Etienne was that she hadn't once asked about the size and number of his estates, or his bank balances. In his wide experience of women, that was a miracle in itself. Unlike the rest of his acquaintances, Gwen spoke to him as though he were an ordinary person and that, Etienne knew, was exactly what he needed. With her as his mistress, he knew he would never be bored again.

Gwen opened her eyes and squinted towards a patch of daylight beyond the window. It must be very early. Dawn was barely brushing the Eastern sky. There was a sweet fragrance in the air she couldn't quite identify. And then she remembered…it was Etienne. She blushed. His arm was still around her. Memories of the hours they had shared came flooding back. She listened to the slow, steady breathing of the man who had taken her body and soul time and again during the hours of darkness. A man who, despite his vast wealth and status, had encouraged her to throw off every one of her inhibitions. If that weren't incredible enough, Gwen knew she would do it again and again, as long as it was with him.

And yet she couldn't stay. He wouldn't want her any more—and in any case, she had to get to work. It wasn't only a thirsty car and an impatient electricity company that worried her. Bankruptcy was staring her in the face. Now she was the sole owner of Le Rossignol, she had to make it pay. Physical need for Etienne fought with her fear of financial ruin. She had left her home in the Welsh valleys so that any mistakes could be made well away from her pessimistic friends and family. Despite their warnings, she had been almost sure this venture would be a success. The only uncertainty had been her business partner, Carys. Now her feather-brained 'friend' was out of the picture, Gwen was doubly determined to make a go of things. But from now on, in those few moments when she wasn't worrying about her fledgling business, she knew she would dream of Etienne.

His breathing was slow and steady. Trying to harden her heart, Gwen began inching herself across the cold expanse of bed, away from him. Her foot had barely been touched by the morning air when Etienne stirred and enveloped her in a firm embrace again.

'Don't tell me you're thinking of getting up so early?'

he murmured. The kiss of his stubble rasped over her skin as he nestled against her shoulder.

'It's light enough for me to walk home and start trying to sort things out.'

'Wait...I'll ring for breakfast,' he said, surfacing fully. 'We have things to discuss.'

'We do?' Gwen asked nervously. Waves of panic uncovered a sense of shame that she had totally cast aside until that moment. She clutched a handful of the thin sheet and buried her face into it. What had she done? What madness had possessed her to surrender everything to a man she had met only a few hours before? Pulling her knees up to her chest, she contracted into a tiny ball of guilt. Mistaking her movement, Etienne released her from his grasp.

'Of course—you'll want to freshen up. There should be everything you need in my bathroom, but if you want anything else, use the bell to call one of my staff.'

'No!' Gwen couldn't bear the thought of total strangers getting the idea she was nothing more than another notch on this man's ego. 'No—thank you. I'll manage.'

He was reaching for his phone, but paused long enough to grab and kiss her before she could scuttle off to the bathroom.

In that instant Gwen knew why she had fallen into his arms so readily. Etienne Moreau was a force of nature, and one she never wanted to resist.

'It's a rare woman who offers to merely "manage" when she could have all my staff running around for her,' he murmured into her hair.

'I've been brought up to take care of myself,' she

said, forcing herself to pull away from his embrace. She kept hold of the sheet as she did so, wrapping it around herself for the journey to the bathroom. Considering the number of times they had made love during the night, there was no point in trying to be modest in front of him, but Gwen needed to make the gesture. Head down, she bolted.

The en-suite was as well stocked as Etienne had said it would be. Gwen found every variety of shower gel from revitalising to relaxing, toothbrushes, a selection of toothpastes and a small but elegant collection of cosmetics. Everything was shrink-wrapped and sealed, as though Etienne's room was in a hotel rather than a private house. The thought that a million other women could have passed this way did nothing for Gwen's self-esteem. When she heard the distant clatter of staff arriving with a breakfast trolley, she hid inside the bathroom until everything went quiet again. She gave it a couple of minutes, and then emerged.

Etienne's bedroom was deserted. Venturing into the lounge, she saw a pair of French doors standing open on the other side of the room. They were draped with curtains of the finest lace and, beyond them, Gwen saw a breakfast table set on a wide balcony. Enough food for two was laid out as a spectacular buffet, complete with starched linen napkins and solid silver cutlery. It was a display Gwen would have studied for ideas if her mind hadn't been full of a more pressing problem—the tall, broad and totally unmistakeable figure pacing back and forth beside it. Etienne was oblivious of the stunning view over the hillside as he spoke into a mobile phone. Even at this distance, he was magnificent. Gwen felt totally out of her depth. She wouldn't have needed the hundreds of family portraits on show downstairs to know he was a born aristocrat. Poise and confidence were obvious in his every word and movement. Despite the intimacy of their night together, at first she could not bear to meet his keen ebony gaze. She concentrated on the only thing she was qualified to do. When he closed his call she took a deep breath and stepped out onto the balcony to join him.

'What would you like for breakfast, *monsieur?*'

As she took a plate from a heated trolley she heard the soft click of his leather-soled shoes on the ancient stones. Then his hand covered hers and he took the plate from her unresisting fingers.

'What happened to "Etienne"? And you aren't one of my staff.' He raised one fine, dark eyebrow in subtle amusement. 'Concentrate on serving yourself, Gwen. I have something very different in mind for you.'

Dragging his gaze away from her, he let it fall onto the breakfast display. As he did so he frowned, as though it was a chore diverting him from something much more pleasurable.

'Try the crêpes. They're the best you'll ever taste.' Lifting a warm croissant onto his own plate, he looked straight back at her.

Gwen took one of the almost transparent pancakes onto her plate. Breakfast with Etienne in his suite was a once-in-a-lifetime experience, but the business part of her brain refused to let go. She felt it was her duty to find out what her customers enjoyed.

'I'll get my chefs to give you their recipe.'

For the first time that morning Gwen's smile was as confident as her reply.

'Thank you. That's very kind, but I'm quite happy with the one I use already. Everyone has their favourites.'

Etienne looked at her carefully. Then he smiled. 'Yes, and I'm no exception. I enjoyed last night, Gwen, as you may have noticed—several times.' His afterthought was a wicked drawl.

Until that moment she had been stealing little glances at him. Now she gave a nervous chuckle and stared resolutely at the breakfast display. Pretending that the choice between berries and syrup was almost as important as his comment, she tried to look cool, calm and composed. It was impossible. Etienne was standing so tall and serene beneath his native sun. She could hardly believe she had spent the night with him.

'In fact, I'd like to make this a more regular arrangement,' he continued.

Gwen had been about to lift a spoonful of fresh fruit salad from a crystal dish. At his words she froze. A droplet of juice trickled down the bowl of the solid silver serving spoon, trembled at its lowest point for a second, and then dropped onto the snowy white tablecloth.

'You want to *what*?' she said faintly.

'I have a lot of things on my mind, Gwen. I need distraction—something to take my mind off it all and restore my faith in human nature. Last night I found the perfect solution, in you. We would make a good team. I'm sure of it. With my support you would be released from all your obligations. There would be no need for you to slave away in a kitchen. You would be free to enjoy life as it should be lived, with no worries.'

She gazed at him, so clearly puzzled that he laughed. When he did that it made her smile, although she still shook her head in bewilderment.

'What do you mean, Etienne?'

'Exactly what I say. I'm so delighted to have found you, *chérie*, it would be my pleasure to provide for you, financially. I don't want you waiting on other people. I want to keep you all to myself, and support you in the way you deserve.'

He was seducing her all over again, simply by using his deliciously accented voice and the promise in those beautiful dark eyes.

Gwen had thought it was impossible for her to be any more nervous. Now the butterflies in her stomach were under attack by a snake of suspicion. She might have been physically innocent when she met Etienne, but growing up with older brothers had given her a basic understanding of the male mind. Preparing for the worst, she hoped for the best and asked slowly,

'Why would you offer me money when we only met last night?'

Taking her free hand, Etienne raised it to his lips and placed a delicate kiss on each of her fingers in turn. Then he looked deep into her eyes and delivered his reply with all the relish of a professional seducer.

'I would have thought that was obvious, *chérie*.'

CHAPTER FOUR

'I want to keep you in my life, Gwen. As my mistress,' Etienne added, since she was looking at him with something close to suspicion. 'Think of the advantages. I could set you up with a restaurant—in Monte Carlo, maybe, where your Michelin-starred menus could dazzle the clientele downstairs while your body delights me in the apartment above…'

His voice was a silken thread, drawing her into his plans. A furious blush began to rise from Gwen's breasts. It was slow to kindle but flared in painful intensity as it reached her cheeks. Dropping the serving spoon with a clatter, she confronted him with eyes as hard as sapphires.

'How dare you? You said our first kiss was an accident. You were right. Anyone can make a mistake, *monsieur*, but it takes a first-class philanderer to build on one and then dress it up with an offer like that!'

He stared at her, totally unable to understand her reaction. 'Gwen? You're upset?'

She glared back at him. 'That's an understatement!'

Still mystified, he gave a particularly Gallic shrug. Acquiring a mistress had never been a problem for him before. Until now, his only difficulty had been tact when ending relationships. Gwen was introducing him to a whole new range of experiences. So far they had all been stellar. This was the first irritation. 'But why should you take offence? It's a perfectly natural arrangement. What's your problem?'

She glared at him. This was unbelievable. She'd just had the most sensuous night of her life and now it was all coming down to money! She felt her fairy tale quickly slipping out of her grasp. 'I don't want anyone controlling me! I ran away from home to escape all that. Now I'm making my own future.'

'You ran away from home?' He looked concerned. 'How long ago was that?'

'Last year.'

That was when Etienne made his next mistake. He smiled. It was a miscalculation, because it did nothing to calm her down and everything to inflame her.

'And *don't* look at me like that! It's not funny. I'm mad at you!'

'You're a grown woman, Gwen. You're too old to run away! Why didn't you simply say you left home?'

'That's not how my family see it,' she said bitterly.

Etienne was on her wavelength immediately. 'Ah… trouble with the relatives?' he said with all the weight of personal experience.

'No—not at all. And that's the problem. My family have always been far too protective for my liking. They've never wanted me to fail, so they've never wanted me to do anything. They want my life to be like them—far too good.'

'That's all I want, too,' Etienne said in a silky voice, reaching for the cafetiere. 'Let's take a seat and discuss this over a coffee.'

'If you're only asking me to be your mistress, then there's nothing to discuss,' Gwen rallied, putting down her plate of crêpes untouched.

'Why not? It's the perfect solution.'

'For you, maybe. You'll have everything you want whenever you want it, with no strings attached.' She could hardly believe what she was saying. All she wanted to do was step back into his arms but, amazed at her own courage and glad of her self-discipline, she was finally finding the courage to stand up for herself.

'How can you say that, *mon amour*?' He looked puzzled. 'As my mistress, you'll benefit from my generosity. You'll have anything and everything you want, too. You can have expense accounts at all the stores you like. I could treat you to a nice little love nest in Paris, *par exemple*. We can live together there whenever I'm in the city. What is your heart's desire? Name it and it's yours. There's no limit.'

Gwen was aghast. 'Well, there's certainly no limit to your nerve! Is there nothing you won't try? Unless it's the idea of making an honest woman of me, as they call it back home.'

He laughed. 'Marriage, you mean? No, I'm afraid that will never be on offer. And there's no need to look so shocked! You've found my Achilles' heel, so the least I can do is to be honest with you. I was nearly caught in that honey trap once before, *chérie*. No woman is going to hold me hostage like that again. You can have absolutely anything you like, except my signature on a marriage certificate.' He chuckled. 'Apart from that one small detail, my generosity knows no limit. Try me. Name your price.'

Reaching for a napkin, Gwen wiped her hands and dropped it onto the table in a symbolic gesture.

'It's nothing you could buy, no matter how much money you've got, *monsieur*. I want my independence, and the chance to make my own way in the world. I don't want to go through life being carried by anyone else.'

Taking a step back, she took one last look at the temptation of him. It was almost impossible to make a stand, he made her body quiver just looking at her, but her principles were at stake. She had to harden her heart.

'I escaped from one gilded cage. I'm not going to let myself be tempted into another. *Au revoir, monsieur.*'

In a swirl of midnight-blue velvet, she was gone.

Etienne never normally wasted time on breakfast. As far as he was concerned, it was something to restore his energy levels after a late night and before an early meeting. That was all. This morning there was a different reason most of his food went untouched. He moved to pour himself a second cup of coffee as Gwen stalked away through his suite. When the door slammed shut behind her, he turned his attention to the beautiful array of food laid out on the table. He didn't normally linger over his selection, but today he had some time to fill. It wouldn't be polite to start eating before Gwen returned. She would come fluttering back to him at any minute in a flurry of tears and apologies. Etienne was quite confident about that. It was what women did.

He had a long wait. When he finally saw Gwen again, she was down in the courtyard. He caught sight of her briefly, storming away from his house with her beautiful dress billowing. She didn't give him a backward glance. Marching down the drive, she disappeared from his sight.

Etienne lowered his eyebrows in silent disapproval. Miss Gwyneth Williams really was one of a kind. This made her the first woman to abandon him of her own accord. *He* was always the one who made the decision to leave. *He* made the first move. *Always.* This was not going to plan. Gwen hadn't even looked back so that he could give her a casual wave, dismissing her from his life for ever. *She didn't give me the satisfaction*, he thought irritably, but his indignation was short-lived. Gwen Williams had satisfied him in quite another way. It was one that would live far longer in his memory. Her mind was her own, but her body must surely be his. He had seen it, and taken her, exactly as he had possessed so many other lovely things that caught his eye.

She couldn't be allowed to snatch it away.

Etienne took his breakfast over to the dining table and sat down in solitary splendour to consider this. As always, the financial press lay beside his place. He usually read it from cover to cover. Today, for the first time in two years, it remained untouched. Instead, he worked his way through far more pastry, crêpes and fruit than he would normally eat.

It was an attempt to distract himself from the enigma

that was Gwen. In her anger, she had revealed some-thing that only made him want her more. Until he'd met her, he had been confident he knew exactly what sort of woman could abandon a happy family. Angela Webbington had shown him how it was done. Yesterday, he had seduced Gwen in the delicious belief she was totally different from his ex-fiancée. Now he didn't know what to make of his little Welsh wonder. Last night she had held him spellbound. This morning, his sweet and tender stranger had shown him a core of iron. He now knew she had the determination to walk away from blood relatives—*family!*—because they cared about her too much.

Etienne shook his head in silent disbelief. If he could continue humouring his stepmother simply because it was his father's dying wish, why couldn't Gwen see how lucky she was? He wondered how it felt to be part of a normal family. The appalling woman who styled herself 'Countess Sophie' continued to dictate shopping lists onto his dead father's exclusive headed notepaper, yet Etienne let her get away with it. That woman was so far beneath his contempt he didn't bother registering his annoyance. Gwen Williams, on the other hand, had run away from something he envied. Etienne's idea of family was people who liked you because they wanted to, not because it was their duty or because they hoped you'd remember them in your will. Why had Gwen run away? From people who wanted her with them? Did she need saving from herself—to be shown how important it was to have people who cared? If she did, he was certainly the man to do just that. It was just a shame she hadn't realised it yet.

She soon would. Etienne was completely confident of that.

Gwen was so furious, she forgot all about her blisters until she reached her front door. There she kicked off her shoes and stood on the still-cool stones while she rummaged for her key. Etienne Moreau was the absolute limit. It had been so perfect last night and then he thought his money could buy everything, including her. She felt insulted. Stamping upstairs, she threw off her beautiful gown. She intended to shrug off that infuriating man in the same movement. It wasn't quite as easy as she hoped. As she pulled on her working clothes it was impossible not to notice how soft and supple his expensive shower gel had left her skin. She lifted her arm and inhaled its heavy, floral perfume again. From that moment on, she would never be able to smell the fragrance of jasmine without being wafted straight back to the luxury of Etienne's suite. And the memory of the night they had shared...

Gwen caught sight of her reflection in her bedroom mirror and it shocked her. Overnight, the vigorous businesswoman who was always so quick to rebuke her from the glass had been replaced. A misty-eyed stranger gazed back at her now.

She jumped straight back to life as a loud knock echoed up from downstairs. There was someone at the door.

'Just a minute!' she called, scrabbling around to collect the unpaid electricity bill, her house keys and bag before flying down to throw open the front door.

It was Etienne. Dressed in another beautifully crafted suit, he pulled off a pair of slick black shades. They flickered in the morning sunlight as he closed the arms and posted them into the top pocket of his jacket. Stunned into silence, Gwen stared at the face she had seen transformed by pleasure such a short, painful time before. He was as unrecognisable as her reflection had been in the mirror upstairs. His eyes showed none of the soft sensuality she remembered so well. They now watched her acutely. The early stubble that had rasped against her naked skin was gone, but his freshly shaved face had lost none of its attraction for her. It made her want to stroke him. If ever a man's body demanded a woman's fingers to peel away his smart façade, it was Etienne's. Despite her fury, Gwen could not help staring. She had an almost overwhelming desire to reach out to him. He had assumed she was dying to become his mistress. He was wrong, but she still wanted to experience the passionate animal lurking beneath his civilised exterior—just not quite so formally…

'You've come to apologise?' she ventured.

That wiped the smile off his face. He grazed his lower lip with his teeth.

'No…what for?' he questioned, mystified.

Gwen was already crimson, but could at least give the appearance of being in control. She hardened her features. He mustn't guess she was thinking about the way his muscles bunched beneath the fine gold skin of his chest. Fidgeting with embarrassment, she blew a stray curl of hair back from her brow with a gust of hot breath.

'You know very well what for, Etienne Moreau.'

He gazed at her, shaking his head. 'No, I don't.'

She stared back. His ebony eyes looked so steady and honest she found it impossible to believe he was goading her. And yet she was being forced into saying words that made her blood boil with embarrassment.

She glared up at him malevolently. 'You tried to buy me. You reduced me to the level of a bowl of bouillabaisse! *You asked me to be your mistress!*' she hissed.

To her total amazement, his response was a confiding chuckle.

'What's the matter with that? As far as I'm concerned, that is one of the greatest compliments a man can pay a woman.'

'Well, it comes pretty low on *my* agenda, I can tell you!' Gwen snapped. The day was already warm, and she was getting hotter by the second.

Etienne managed to stop smiling, but could not hide the relish in his eyes. 'That isn't how it felt to me, last night,' he murmured.

Gwen struggled to hang onto the remains of her self-control. If only he weren't looking at her like that, all flashing dark eyes and lupine grin. It was all she could do not to cave in and smile back.

That would be disastrous. She had principles at stake. They had forced her to walk away from him once. To run back into his arms now would show him how vulnerable she was. She hadn't escaped from the claustrophobia of home to get locked into a relationship that would die with the speed of his enthusiasm.

'Fine—we've established that you're totally unrepentant. So what makes you think you can hunt me down in my own home? I've told you, I'm not interested in your shabby little offer. If you're not here to deliver an apology, would you mind telling me why you *are* here?' she snapped.

As she spoke she caught sight of her car. It was standing on the terrace, in the shade of the gnarled old golden rain tree. She stopped. Her glance flicked from Etienne's face to the Citroen, and back again. There was absolutely no trace of amusement in his expression now. Annoyance spoke loudly in his every movement as he pulled her keys from his pocket and thrust them towards her.

'I came to return your car.'

His voice was full of contempt. It was nothing compared to the awful crawling shame that slithered over Gwen in an agony of embarrassment.

'Oh...er, yes...of course!' Desperately she looked down at her bag, rifling through tissues, receipts, lipstick, foreign coins and parking permits. 'How much do I owe you?' she muttered.

'Stop!' he said in a voice that instantly commanded her full attention. Looking up, she winced as his eyes inflicted points of pure pain.

'I wouldn't dream of insulting you again with talk of money, Gwyneth. Consider it my pleasure,' he said through a smile that showed all his teeth, but not in a good way.

Gwen opened her mouth to reply, but he was already on his way, shaking off her wordless outrage. She watched him storm away in total silence, fighting the urge to call him back. Maybe this was for the best. It was hard to know which was worse. A man who couldn't admit he was in the wrong—or a debt that he wouldn't let her repay.

She knew both would work on her like grit in an oyster.

Fury propelled Etienne down the hill in silence. Two rebuffs in as many hours were unknown. What on earth had he been thinking about, laying himself open to such an attack? As he strode through the great gates of his chateau he wondered what had come over him. This wasn't how it was supposed to work. The thought of never seeing Gwen again worked on him like a headache. If he picked up a girl, they had a good time and when the evening was over, so was the liaison.

The only exception to that rule had been Angela. They had fitted together so perfectly it would have been a sin not to take it further. Old money and new ideas, 'tellystocracy' and the real thing combined in the most beautiful couple in the public eye. They had been so perfectly matched, it had been a nightmare. One word had kept coming back to haunt him. Duty. Celebrity anchorwoman Angela could not understand why she should respect the Moreau family and its traditions. That had spawned a million arguments, but the final crowbar forcing Etienne and Angela apart had been far smaller, and totally innocent...

The memory of the day he discovered Angela's worst deception still had the power to pierce Etienne like a barb. Gwen Williams was obsessed by her career. In that respect she was exactly like Angela Webbington. Why should he be surprised if both women were cut from the same fabric? With a snort he decided it was madness to have considered making Gwen his mistress. A short affair was one thing. Offering to restrict himself to one woman for an unspecified length of time was quite another. They always put themselves first and others nowhere. One tragic error of judgement in his life was surely enough of a warning.

It had taken Etienne a long time to start getting over that. And now there was Gwen.

He marched on. The sun was rising higher in the sky by the moment, but Etienne would have been at boiling point if it had been January. He had never lacked for anything in his life, and he wasn't about to start denying himself now. Whatever happened, he was going to have Miss Gwyneth Williams.

He stopped—why was she playing on his mind so much? Was it simply because he couldn't have her, or because she was something special—? No, he baulked at using that word. It was too loaded with meaning. She was *totally unlike* any other woman he had ever met. That made her...

He gazed along the drive towards his impressive chateau, trying to think of a description.

Unique. Yes, that was it. He smiled. She had shown no signs of fawning around his money. Quite the opposite. She had stood up for herself. He couldn't help contrasting her behaviour with Angela. His ex-fiancée had made a career out of defying him for the hell of it, and the headlines.

He continued on towards his home, but this time more slowly. Maybe there were faults on both sides. If he had given Gwen time to cool off properly, they might have laughed about their argument. It would have been forgiven in an instant. The making up would have been a lot slower, and supremely enjoyable. He liked that idea. Gwen had a lovely laugh. That wasn't the only thing he enjoyed about her. She pleased his body in a way more experienced women had never managed. Gwen, in all her innocence, was a superbly generous lover. He remembered how responsive his body had been to her touch, and her delight in it. The simple act of thinking about her made him want her, right here and now. He turned in a crunch of gravel and took two long strides back towards her house. Then he stopped. Striking while her anger was hot had made her reject his offer a few minutes before. It obviously wasn't the way to tame her. A woman like Gwen deserved careful handling.

For once, Etienne would have to make haste slowly.

With a smile, he strolled back home to plan his next move.

Gwen's embarrassment was so total she thought she would never recover. She could have cooked crêpes on her cheeks. Etienne had been doing her a favour, but she had yelled first without even bothering to ask questions. She had wrecked any hope of seeing him ever again. It was the worst disappointment she had ever suffered— and when her staff clocked into work at the restaurant, it got a whole lot worse.

'And don't forget, the Count of Malotte is booked in for lunch today!' Clemence the waitress nudged Gwen archly.

'I had no idea, but I doubt if he'll turn up,' Gwen said grimly. 'He's probably had enough of my kind of hospitality to last him a lifetime.'

She was wrong on both counts. Etienne was determined to taste it again—but on his own terms. The first volley of his attack on her will power arrived shortly before lunch that morning. Gwen was busy in the kitchen. Suddenly there was a commotion out in the restaurant. Wiping her hands on a cloth, she rushed out in time to see three large, flat cardboard boxes being unloaded from a florists' van. The delivery man handed her an expensive, tissue-lined envelope and—more importantly as far as Gwen was concerned—an invoice with the word 'paid' stamped across it in large, comforting letters.

She tore open the envelope. It contained a short note written in real ink on handmade paper. She knew who it was from without needing to see the bold, flowing signature at the bottom. The faintest trace of Etienne's sophisticated aftershave had been enough to get her pulses racing.

Dear Gwen,
It would be pointless to send flowers to you at home. You obviously spend all your time at Le Rossignol, so I've arranged to have regular deliveries of fresh flowers sent to the restaurant from now on. That way you can appreciate them. There will be a bouquet for each table, and a complimentary corsage of miniature orchids for each female diner—

'So? What do you think?'

Gwen jumped at the interruption. It was a deliciously familiar voice. She looked up, and found herself gazing straight into the beautiful brown eyes of Etienne Moreau.

'I think you're full of surprises.' She folded the letter and carefully replaced it in its envelope. Then she slid it into her apron pocket. 'Thank you, Etienne. It's far more than I deserve. I can't tell you how sorry I am for the misunderstanding earlier,' she muttered, after checking none of her staff were close enough to hear.

He waved away her apology. 'Oh, this is inconsequential. It's a simple gesture, nothing more.'

He couldn't have been more wrong as far as Gwen was concerned. It meant all the world to her. No man had ever sent her flowers before. She looked up at him with shining eyes, but he hadn't finished.

'I knew a hard-headed businesswoman like you wouldn't want money wasted.' He went on, before she could interrupt. 'This way my honour is satisfied, and you get a unique selling point for your restaurant.'

With that simple phrase, her newly revived dreams melted like candyfloss in a heatwave. The ulterior motive behind his gift robbed it of all romance. Gwen put on a brave face and tried not to care. She only had her own temper to blame, after all. It was too late for regrets.

'Ah, so they aren't a sign of your affection. They're for the good of your conscience and my restaurant!' She tried to chuckle, but it was difficult while she was so busy trying to swallow her disappointment.

'Yes, and I can do Le Rossignol another good turn too,' he said with satisfaction. 'I have a business proposition to put to you, Gwen. When I've finished lunching here, you can come back to my yacht with me and we'll discuss it.'

'Today?' she enquired, leading him to his table.

'Of course. Good ideas won't wait.'

'But it will have to…we've got another big party here tonight. I've got to supervise everything!'

Etienne was unfazed. He sat down and watched with interest as Gwen's staff began unpacking the flowers and putting them out on display. 'That's not a problem—I'll send a couple of my chefs down from the chateau. They can cover for you.'

Gwen gaped at him. 'No—I don't think so! This restaurant is my life. I can't abandon it on a whim!'

Etienne clicked his tongue in disgust. 'If this place is so important to you, you can spare a couple of hours to consider its future.'

'It wouldn't have a future if I hadn't mortgaged myself to the hilt. I can't let my guard down for a minute, much less go gallivanting off on a private yacht for the afternoon! And me on a yacht? What on earth would my old mam and dad say?'

'If they had any sense, they'd tell you to do as I say,' Etienne said mildly.

Gwen was aghast. She couldn't possibly leave it at that. Hands on hips, she regarded him, her head on one side.

'I thought you were issuing me with an invitation, not an order?'

He raised a mocking brow. 'I was. You don't have to come, but you would be crazy not to hear what I have to say.'

'In your opinion,' she said caustically, but her suspicion had no effect on Etienne. He was far too sure of himself.

'You'll be of the same opinion, when you've listened to me.'

Gwen pulled out the chair beside him and sat down. 'All right—if your idea is so good, tell me about it now.'

He shook his head. 'All the relevant paperwork is set out in my conference room aboard *The Windflower*. You'll see it this afternoon.'

'No, I won't, because I shan't be there. I'll be here,' she explained patiently. 'I've told you. I must supervise arrangements for the party.'

A small wrinkle appeared between Etienne's brows. He took a sip of mineral water, which gave him time to iron out his frown. 'I'm giving you the opportunity of several lifetimes, and you want to delay things? I thought you couldn't wait?' He looked at her narrowly.

'I *can't* wait, but I *must*,' she stated.

He turned slightly in his seat, studying her for some time before replying.

'A good manager knows how to delegate,' he said eventually.

Gwen was glad he sounded reasonable rather than irritated, but it still took courage to state her case.

'Maybe: but I'm not just a manager. I'm the owner, head cook and bottle-washer. There is no fallback position. It's me. Although,' she added quickly, raising her hand to stop him objecting, 'I *might* be able to get away tomorrow. Le Rossignol is closed for our half-day. I usually spend the time stocktaking and going through the accounts. If your offer of some temporary help right now still stands…' she ventured, looking up at him from beneath her long, dark lashes. He gave a brief nod.

'I *could* try and get everything done today, so I've got tomorrow afternoon free.'

'Then I suppose that will have to do.' He returned her look with interest. 'I'll send a car to pick you up, then, after lunch. It wouldn't do to have you run out of petrol again, would it?'

She flushed in embarrassment. Until that moment she had been totally unable to tear her gaze away from him. Now her eyes were glad to have an excuse to escape.

'Tell me—did you drive my car back to the *gîte* yourself this morning?' she said in a low voice.

'Of course.' He shrugged as though the gesture was nothing. But to Gwen, secretly, it meant a lot—that he'd gone out of his way for her. Then he checked his watch with a deftness of touch she remembered so well, and Gwen signalled for his menu to be brought. As he studied it her mind was a jangle of possibilities. After the way she had spoken to him earlier, seduction must be the very last thing on his mind. His businesslike attitude just seemed to confirm this. Still, he was here and she could at least try to make amends. Wistfully, she realised he would be highly unlikely to pull her in out of her depth, ever again.

He looked so calm now, Gwen began to doubt her sanity. They had tumbled through the night, she had snubbed him, stormed off and then snubbed him a second time, yet there was absolutely no trace of their history on his face or in his manners. Both were as perfect as ever.

'Thank you for sorting out my car. It's fine now,' she said uncomfortably, hoping his staff hadn't told him of her simple stupidity in letting it run dry.

'As good as any old vehicle can be,' he allowed. 'My mechanics gave it a full service. Then I filled it up with petrol. She'll be good for a while longer.'

Gwen gasped. 'Oh, I must owe you a fortune!' She couldn't believe he'd had to take her car to the filling station for her—it was all so embarrassing.

He looked equally shocked. 'Of course not. It was all done on site at my chateau. There's no charge. Once the problem had been identified, my people did a few little repairs and a spot of touching up. After that, I said I'd test-drive it for them.'

'And did you?'

'Only as far as your *gite*, as it turned out. I was intending to drive you down to Le Rossignol.'

That revived something of Gwen's fighting spirit. '*You* were going to drive me in *my* car?' she asked pointedly.

Etienne struggled visibly to bite back a smile at her indignation.

'You are a remarkable woman, Gwen,' he drawled. 'Last night was a unique experience. I feel privileged to have been part of your life, if only for a few hours.'

Watching him skate on a veneer of perfect manners made her feel totally inadequate. If he was struggling to ignore the bad feeling that had passed between them, then perhaps she should, too. Gripping the edge of her chair, she wondered what to say. Surely if he really considered her mistress material he would have bundled her straight back to bed first thing that morning. Staring across the table at him now, she saw no trace of the wild beast who had ravished her time and again through the hours of darkness. Now he was reduced to the status of a normal executive, lunching at his favourite restaurant. *Reduced*? Gwen almost laughed out loud at that idea. Etienne Moreau was unique, to use his own word. His effect could never be lessened in any way. Beneath those beautiful clothes he had the body of a god and the bearing of a count. Turning down his offer had been close to impossible. It was only her self-esteem that had made her do it. Now she wasn't sure how much restraint she had left.

'You're right. Last night was wonderful.' She passed the tip of her tongue nervously over her lips, remembering. He noticed, and relented slightly. She saw it in his smile. Almost immediately, his expression was shadowed with regret. Gwen found she had to look away. She took refuge behind a sharp, businesslike tone.

'But this is today, Etienne. Now, if you would excuse me, you're quite right. I must get back to work. Sex and business don't mix.'

CHAPTER FIVE

SHE had meant to walk straight out of the door in a businesslike manner, but made the mistake of looking back at him. She was immediately caught in Etienne's gaze. His velvety brown eyes had softened dangerously and were sparkling with mischief. 'How would you know, Gwen? I was your first—and if you let me have my way, I'll be the only man you'll ever need.'

His smile was slow, seductive and totally irresistible.

'You're awfully sure of yourself, Etienne.' And with good reason, she thought with a sigh. She turned to leave, unable to bear the infuriating temptation of him any more. Etienne raised his dark brows in a warning gesture.

'Experience can't be denied.' His voice had all the depth and intensity of crushed cacao, but it brought Gwen no comfort at all.

'That's what worries me. You have a track record, I have none—or at least I didn't until I met you,' she said, feeling a flush run over her cheeks and wishing she didn't blush quite so easily. Etienne was far too self-confident to need any encouragement. 'I'd like to keep it that way, thanks, until I find a man who thinks the same way as I do.'

'I thought I did. Until we met, I lived in the present and looked to the future. The past was no good to me. Haven't you said as much yourself, in abandoning your family to come here to Malotte?'

His innocent smile made her suspicious. 'Are you suggesting that meeting me has changed your outlook on life?' she said warily. Etienne's smile spoke for him. He was lulling her into a false sense of security with warm brown eyes and a knowing expression. He was charming, he was delightful, and she wished with all her heart that he could be hers.

Her heart in her mouth, she waited. Etienne stayed silent.

Eventually, her nerve broke.

'Well, I can't hang around here all day—'

'No other woman could have—'

They had started to speak at exactly the same time. Gwen stared at him. What on earth had he been about to say?

'Go on,' she said faintly.

'No…I interrupted you. You're right, Gwen. I should let you get back to work. Carry on and I'll see you tomorrow,' he said with graceful insistence.

Gwen let her eyes rest on his face. He was lovely, but she had to pack up all her fantasies in a cast-iron trunk and head back to real life. This wasn't the time to feel angry, embarrassed or ashamed. It was an opportunity to imprint every nuance of Etienne upon her mind, for from this moment on their relationship had to stay on a purely business footing.

'Why are you staring at me like that?' he said, without looking up.

'Because I'm waiting to take your order, of course,' Gwen improvised quickly, pulling the pantry notebook from the pocket of her apron.

'I'd rather you left your staff to deal with that side of things. As I said, I've got something far more interesting on offer for you, Gwen.' He paused. 'I was going to wait till tomorrow, so that I could have all the financial documents for you to look at, but I want to offer you a business proposition—nothing more. I have visited Le Rossignol often enough to know that your restaurant would benefit from serious investment, and I have been thoroughly impressed by what this place has to offer.'

Gwen's mouth fell open. 'Are you offering me money again?' she said faintly.

'Not in that way!' He laughed. 'This would be a strictly business arrangement, binding on both sides. I don't waste money, Gwen. You have made your feelings clear earlier, and now I'm making mine clear. I'd like to invest in Le Rossignol.'

If anyone needed financial help, it was Gwen. Etienne Moreau was clearly more than just sex on legs. He knew how to use all his attributes to the best effect, and not simply his body. She was tempted instantly. How could she not be? This might be a solution to all her problems. Her first reaction was to reach out and hug him. She stopped herself just in time. This was *just* business! Any kind of physical contact with him might push her over that precipice of temptation again. Instead, she pressed her hands to her cheeks in delight.

'Etienne…are you really sure you want to do this?'

'I've told you—when it comes to my best interests I look to the future, rather than dwelling on the past.'

Gwen let her breath go in a great gasp.

'Wait until you see my offer before you commit yourself,' he warned, but his smile had a playful twinkle she had never noticed before.

Gwen's world was spinning. A few bittersweet hours ago this man had stripped her of all her inhibitions. She wasn't going to show him how he could still affect every fibre of her being.

Gwen set off early for work next morning. Her car's interior was already baking. She was so distracted by thoughts of her meeting with Etienne, she started fiddling with its air-conditioning straight away. It hadn't worked for months, but within seconds a cool breeze was rippling around the car. Etienne had worked a miracle. But then her core temperature began to rise. It looked as if she would have to fight on several fronts to stop him filling her mind completely, but he was proving to be as useful as he was charming. She smiled. Lounging around on a yacht while he talked business sounded close to heaven. She would have to keep her professional hat jammed well down over her eyes to stop the seductive Monsieur Moreau feeding her emotional candyfloss. She was going to make this work! He'd respected her decision not to become his mistress, and now he was treating her like a professional.

She impressed on everyone that she was determined to take the afternoon off, for once. It worked like magic. Lunch was cleared away in record time. After that, all she had to do was wait for the car Etienne had promised. That was the worst part. Each time she checked the time, the hands of her watch had hardly moved. Desperate that no one should see who was picking her up from work, Gwen let her staff leave early. Only minutes after she let the last one out the back door, a chauffeur arrived at the front.

Suddenly her whole body was alight with fear. What would happen when she was alone with Etienne again—on a yacht?

Slinging her bag over her shoulder, she strode out into the sunlight. She wasn't carrying much, but it gave her something to do with her hands. It was hard to look confident when her nerves were stretched to breaking point. The chauffeur swung the car door open for her. She was faintly alarmed to find Etienne seated inside. This was a test, but it wasn't as worrying as it might have been. She had been scared of making a fool of herself by trying the wrong door, or failing to get it open. Now she could step inside with confidence.

'You were ready and waiting?' He sounded impressed.

Gwen relaxed a little more. *This might not be such an ordeal after all,* she thought, trying to forget the last of her fears. She settled back in the expensively fragrant seat.

'Of course. How long is this meeting likely to take?' she said briskly. Out of the corner of her eye she saw Etienne raise his eyebrows.

'That depends—although as you've already broken

my rule about answering back, the prospects don't look good.' He shot a sideways glance at her—full of mischief.

Gwen steeled her resolve and ignored his teasing. 'Why don't you outline your idea to me now? That would save time. It's a shame we didn't discuss it fully yesterday in my office, as I suggested.'

'No, it isn't. That's your workplace. People are in and out all the time, asking questions and dragging you away at irregular intervals. If I took you to a rival establishment for lunch you'd spend more time dissecting their menu than listening to me. Also, I have the yacht—why not mix business with pleasure and take you out to sea?'

Gwen gave him a calculating look. 'As long as you aren't taking me for a ride as well.'

A familiar wicked smile spread over his face. 'Oh, no,' he said, adding after a suggestive pause, 'Not *this* time.'

There was hardly any time to enjoy the sensation of riding in Etienne's luxurious car. In only a few minutes it drew to a halt outside the Hotel Splendide and the chauffeur leapt out to help her from the car.

'You've changed your plans already, Etienne? I didn't think you'd really take me onto your yacht, but this makes up for it!' She gazed up at the magnificent building, trying to take in every aspect of the luxurious hotel and its hordes of uniformed staff.

'Make the most of it. We're not staying here. There's a helicopter waiting for us on the roof.'

Gwen was horrified. 'Etienne! You can't just walk

through a place like this and expect to use their helicopter!'

He was dismissive. 'Of course I can. It's my hotel,
and my helicopter. *The Windflower* is moored offshore,
well away from prying eyes and long lenses.'

They were wafted up to the roof in an elevator that
was as silent as it was smooth. Etienne escorted her out
onto the roof. Gwen was nervous as the pilot helped her
into her seat and fastened the seat belt. Nothing like this
had ever happened to her before. However, after a
moment of fear as they lifted off, she slowly began to
relax. The bustle of the world below faded away as they
zoomed towards the sea. She had no sooner decided she
liked the sensation of flying in a helicopter than they
began circling in to land on the deck of an enormous
ocean-going yacht, moored far out in the bay.

'I didn't think it was possible for your eyes to get any
bigger, Gwen!' Etienne smiled. He moved as though he
was about to lay his hand on her shoulder, but pulled it
away at the last moment.

'It's enormous—and so beautiful!' She sighed,
gazing down into the perfect blue of the on-board pool.
'However much must it have cost?'

It would have been an obvious comment to make to
any of her friends from the valley back at home, but the
worst sort of social gaffe in the circumstances. Her
hands flew to her mouth.

'Oh, Etienne, how rude was *that!* I'm so sorry!'

He chuckled indulgently. 'Don't be. Your honesty
sends a real breath of fresh air through my life, Gwen.
Any other woman would have pretended to be gazing

FREE BOOKS OFFER

To get you started, we'll send you
2 FREE books and a FREE gift

There's no catch, everything is **FREE**

Accepting your 2 **FREE** books and **FREE** mystery gift
places you under no obligation to buy anything.

Be part of the Mills & Boon® Book Club™ and receive your favourite
Series books up to 2 months before they are in the shops and delivered
straight to your door. Plus, enjoy a wide range of **EXCLUSIVE** benefits!

- Best new women's fiction – delivered right to
  your door with FREE P&P

- Avoid disappointment – get your books up to
  2 months before they are in the shops

- No contract – no obligation to buy

We hope that after receiving your free books you'll
want to remain a member. But the choice is yours.
So why not give us a go? You'll be glad you did!

Visit **millsandboon.co.uk** to stay up to date
with offers and to sign-up for our newsletter

2 **FREE** books
and a
FREE gift

P0EIA

Mrs/Miss/Ms/Mr   Initials

BLOCK CAPITALS PLEASE

Surname

Address

Postcode

Email

MILLS & BOON

DETACH AND POST CARD TODAY!

The Mills & Boon® Book Club™ – Here's how it works:

Accepting your free books places you under no obligation to buy anything. You may keep the books and gift and return the despatch note marked "cancel". If we do not hear from you, about a month later we'll send you 4 brand new books priced at £3.19* each. That is the complete price – there is no extra charge for post and packaging. You may cancel at any time, otherwise we will send you 4 stories a month which you may purchase or return to us – the choice is yours.

*Terms and prices subject to change without notice.

NO STAMP NEEDED!

MILLS & BOON®
Book Club

FREE BOOK OFFER
FREEPOST NAT 10298
RICHMOND
TW9 1BR

NO STAMP
NECESSARY
IF POSTED IN
THE U.K. OR N.I.

into my eyes while her mind calculated my net worth. Business associates would assume it was leased. The truth is *The Windflower* is all mine. But when it comes to how much she costs—well…' he gave another of his characteristic shrugs '…it would be rude to discuss it. As I've told you before, I value my privacy highly. When I discovered that there are a thousand tiny, uninhabited tropical islands scattered around the world, it was a challenge I couldn't resist. I contacted a designer and asked him to build me a vessel that provided seven-star accommodation. He did the work, all I did was sign the cheques. Whatever she cost, she's worth every cent. Whenever I get some free time, I head out to sea. For those occasions when my companion doesn't feel like sharing a hammock slung between two palm trees, I can whisk them back to my ship on the launch or by helicopter, depending how far out she's moored. As a floating pleasure palace, she's invaluable.'

As he spoke he leaned across her, so close she could feel the warmth of his face next to hers. A mad impulse made her want to kiss his cheek, but she resisted. He kept his eyes resolutely fixed on his beautiful yacht, but Gwen guessed he was waiting for her to make a move. He was so sure of himself, it made her even more determined not to let herself be swept away by the rip tide of her desire. The half-smile sculpting his beautiful mouth dared her to go back on her word and give in to his every temptation. After stalking out of his house in such fury, she couldn't possibly back down. She drew in one long, slow, lingering breath. It was filled with the high notes of his cedar-fragranced aftershave. That was delicious enough, but beneath it simmered the warmer, darker temptations of vital maleness.

'I'll bet your lifetime list of islands has a column for women, too,' she murmured, finding it hard to sound sarcastic when he was so very close.

'It's a hobby,' he said with a mischievous grin.

The helicopter drifted into land exactly on the target painted in the middle of its upper deck. As the rotors slowed to a halt a long procession of Etienne's domestic staff emerged. They greeted her with smiles as he introduced each of them by name. Gwen had been nervous. Now she felt much more relaxed as Etienne showed her down from the deck. The contrast between hot bright sunshine and the cool silence of the luxurious living conditions was like chilled champagne.

'This is lovely,' she sighed. Her sleeveless T-shirt was no protection against the midday sun. She was glad of the cold kiss of air-conditioning on the tender pink skin of her shoulders. 'It's even better than your hotel.'

'I should hope so. And this is only the offices and boardrooms. The suites are situated where they get the best views.'

Everything had a brand-new sheen about it. Gwen wanted to run her fingers over the polished, turned wood of handrails or the sleek chrome and glass fittings. Each time they passed an open door, she couldn't resist peeking in. Etienne clearly did a lot of entertaining. There were several lounges and public areas, all decorated with restrained good taste. Everything had the look of money well spent—a lot of money. The only thing the place lacked was people.

'Where is everyone? You've got dozens of staff on here—I've seen them. Where are they now?'

'In a ship this size it is easy to disappear. That's why I like it so much.' He ran his hand along a polished rosewood rail. Gwen saw real pride in his movements, and satisfaction in his smile. 'I can slip away from the largest party, and everyone will assume I'm merely circulating in some other part of the yacht.'

'It sounds like you enjoy socialising about as much as I do,' she joked.

'No, I hate it.'

He was deadly serious. So was Gwen.

'Snap.'

'I can't believe that.' His expression eased, as though the ice had been broken and he was glad neither of them had fallen through. 'You were born to entertain, Gwen, if anyone ever was.'

His voice was like satin now. With blinding insight, Gwen knew he was calling to mind the way she had pleased him in bed. Her mind filled with unforgettable images, too, but she wasn't going to fall under his spell again. Her first experience had given him the impression she was his mistress for the asking, and that made her wary. She wasn't going to let him take advantage of her so easily this time. Her self-esteem depended on it.

'Your staff didn't turn a hair when you introduced me. I suppose they're used to you bringing an endless procession of women on board,' she said, reminding herself that spectacular skills like his weren't honed over one night, or even a thousand.

Etienne had an easy answer. 'The reason for that is simple. They know you're here on business.'

Gwen laughed. 'When their boss has your taste for the ladies? The staff here must have seen a thousand different ones. I'll bet they're all discussing exactly what sort of "business" we're up to right now!'

'Gwen!' Etienne looked shocked as he showed her into a boardroom and flipped the sign outside to 'In Conference'. 'They wouldn't dream of it, if they wanted to keep their jobs. I hope you don't allow that sort of gossip in your kitchens at Le Rossignol!'

'Of course I don't. My staff don't have time to look up from their work. Nattering about anything is right out of the question.'

Trying to forget all the gossip she had heard about the Countess Sophie's plans for Etienne, she followed close behind him. He led the way into a light, airy room furnished with high-tech screens and projectors. A long, highly polished table stood in the centre, surrounded by chairs. A crystal carafe of iced water and two glasses stood beside a blotting pad placed at the head of the table. Gwen also noticed a small collection of official-looking documents. Etienne strode towards his place and pulled out the grand carved chair nearest it. He gestured for her to sit down. As she did he poured a glass of water and placed it on a coaster beside her.

'I thought you would be too sensible to allow chit-chat to distract your staff. It's another sign of a good businesswoman. The other night I saw how much you hate to disappoint your customers.'

That wicked smile was dancing around his handsome

mouth again. Gwen stared at him, willing herself not to blush. It didn't work.

Taking his seat at the head of the table, he opened the file that lay on top of the pile before him. She watched his eyes scan the first page, wishing he would look at her. When he did, she was unprepared for the effect it would have. Her blush returned with increasing heat. The urge to move in her seat with the memory of squirming beneath his hands fired her with a desire she knew she could never risk tasting again.

'It's true, any visitor to Le Rossignol can be sure their privacy will be respected,' Gwen said, trying to settle herself. Despite everything, the amusement in his eyes was infectious. Her façade of disapproval cracked with a smile, but she was determined to keep this business meeting on track. 'Any secret is totally safe with me.'

'I knew it would be. That's good. I'd prefer our discussions here today to remain confidential,' he said, and then dropped his voice to a seductive whisper. Leaning forward, he smiled at her with a warmth that threatened to melt the core of her resistance.

'The fact is, I'm hoping to make you an offer you can't refuse, Gwen Williams.'

Her eyes widened with alarm. If he was making a move on her, she would be powerless to resist. They were miles out to sea. There could be no escape this time. Terrified he would trample all over her feelings again, Gwen knew she must resist. She also knew it would be far too great a test of her will power. Her body was urging her to stay, and melt into his arms again. It was left to her mind to try and save her self-respect.

Dropping her hands flat on the boardroom table, she tried to spring to her feet. Quickly, Etienne dropped his hand over hers. It was a heavy, decisive movement with no trace of seduction or romance. She froze, and looked into his eyes. They were glowing, but with nothing more than cold reason.

'Relax! I've told you before. It isn't that sort of offer, Gwen.'

Slowly, she sank back into her seat. His message was received and understood. She looked down at her reflection in the mirror-like sheen of the boardroom table. For some time Etienne didn't move a muscle. Then slowly he withdrew his hand, dragging his slightly roughened palm across the smooth, delicate skin of her fingers. Picking up his pen, he switched his attention to a report on his blotter. While Gwen waited in silence, he made some notes. The sound of his gold nib inscribed the silence. When it seemed he had forgotten her, she lifted her palms slowly from the table, ready to put them in her lap. She was mortified to see they left prints behind on the polished surface. They lasted only as long as the pressure of his hand had done on her skin. *His memory of our night together must have vanished in the same way,* she thought.

Etienne continued to study the open file before him. When he sensed she had settled again, he looked up from his notes. His expression had all the integrity of jet. It combined beauty and inescapable darkness in one irresistible look.

'I'll come straight to the point, Gwen. I need to broaden my investment portfolio. The hospitality industry is exactly the type of diversification I need. Le

Rossignol has been my favourite restaurant from the moment Nick bought it. I've since discovered its success is entirely due to your flair in the kitchen. I'd hate to see it close through lack of working capital. That's why I want to inject some money into your business.' He paused minutely as Gwen opened her mouth to interrupt. The look on his face dared her to disagree. Taking her cue from his expression, she said nothing, but smiled instead.

Etienne looked back at his notes and reconsidered. Clearing his throat, he rephrased his last words. 'I want to ensure I can dine there whenever I like, safe in the knowledge that you are going to be the hostess and head of the kitchen. In short, Le Rossignol needs money, and I have plenty of it. Funds would be the only thing on offer—it's no good expecting me to lend a hand with the washing-up,' he coaxed her with a smile.

Gwen tried to respond, but she could barely form a reply. 'If you know so much about the money side, I'm amazed you aren't ready to employ someone for little details like that,' she said faintly.

'Talking about the work is the extent of my skill in the kitchen,' he replied with dry humour. 'That's why you will remain in complete control. I've had my experts draw up a legal document—this is your copy.' He closed the file he had been working on and slid it across the table to her. 'Where they've been too pompous I've added a few foot-notes so that you and I both know exactly what they mean.'

Gwen stared at the orange file as though it were a snake ready to strike. How could anyone put money into a business without wanting to control it?

'Th-thank you, Etienne. That's very kind of you,'

she said slowly, hoping she really could believe that. She had been brought up by hard-nosed business people. She knew what business life did to people, and couldn't bear to think of Etienne being similarly underhand. 'But I have to ask—what's in this for you?'

'I've told you: it is part of my wider strategy to spread my investments. In addition, I get to eat and entertain at the finest venue in this part of France.'

'And that's all?' She watched him carefully. He showed no outward signs of tension whatsoever. Leaning forward, he clasped his hands loosely on the desk before him. He was the perfect businessman, ready for the next topic on his agenda.

'What happens if I say no?'

He stared at her, taking some time to compute what she had said. Then without warning he broke eye contact, poured himself a glass of water and took a long, slow drink. When he put down his glass, he stretched the silence further until eventually he announced: 'If you do, you will prove yourself to be as sadly misguided as the last woman who refused to take my advice. I'm sure you know what happened to her.'

Gwen felt her stomach turn a somersault. In a couple of days, Etienne had flipped her life upside down to devastating effect. When she looked at him now, her eyelids fluttered with apprehension. In contrast, his gaze was rock steady. Penetrating her puny defences, his single-minded power alarmed her. She passed the tip of her tongue nervously over her parched lips.

'I hardly like to ask,' she said faintly. Etienne looked surprised, and suspicious.

'You must have seen the press coverage at the time?'

Gwen shook her head, confused. His laughter subsided into a bitter smile.

'It was front-page news. The glossies had a field day.'

Gwen, who couldn't remember when she last had the time to read anything beyond a recipe book, stared at him bleakly.

'Thank you for your discretion, Gwen, but don't worry about hurting my feelings. I no longer have any. They were burned away long ago. Angela Webbington's deceit made sure of that. And with your links to Nick, I'm sure he's told you all the repulsive details the media missed.'

'No…I hardly know the man.' She shook her head, bewildered. 'He's my landlord, that's all. Since Carys jilted him and I bought out their share of the business, we've rarely had time to chat.'

Etienne stared at her for a long time. Gwen felt under intense pressure, but she could do nothing about it. She had never heard of this Angela Webbington in her life, but she was certain of one thing. The moment she next got her hands on a computer, search engines would be humming with the name.

'There's no point in expecting me to crack and change my story, Etienne. I can only tell you the truth. I have no idea what went on in your past. And I'm not sure I want you to tell me, right now,' she said uneasily. 'I'd rather feel free to come to my own decision over your plan. I don't want the shadow of some other woman's mistake hanging over me.'

His expression changed, but she found it impossible to tell what was going on in his mind.

'Then you're very wise,' he said quietly. 'Let's concentrate on my plans to become your business partner, instead. What do you think, Miss Williams?' he said, gently mocking her earnest expression.

Gwen took a deep breath. She felt on safer ground when the talk turned to Le Rossignol, but had to speak her mind. The chances were Etienne wouldn't like that, and she didn't relish the thought of provoking him.

'I—I shall have to think about it,' she ventured, too afraid of what she might see to lift her eyes from the smart, customised file in front of her. Then she thought of a way to escape from this confrontation with her dignity intact. 'Can I take this away with me and study it? I could give you my answer tomorrow.'

He was silent for so long, Gwen couldn't stand it. Finally she let her eyes work their way across the table until she reached his blotting pad. His hands were there, as smooth and golden as ever. They cradled the barrel of his fountain pen as lightly as they had once danced over her body. Now they were still. Her gaze was drawn inexorably upwards, over the body she craved to his resolute stare. It was softer now, but still warned her to keep at arm's length.

'Is that all right? Can I have some time to consider your offer?' she repeated nervously. He pressed his lips together. It was a gesture of exclusion, concealing every trace of their naturally sensuous shape.

'I can't deny I'm surprised, Gwen. I thought you'd jump at the chance. But you can certainly take time to read over the contract—of that I insist.'

'I didn't come this far to sign away everything I'm

fighting for in a moment of desperation— I mean, *to sign away all my rights without studying what my responsibilities will be,*' she corrected herself quickly.

Etienne raised a brow at the word she had been swift to cover up. 'Desperate, Gwen?'

There was no point in denying it. This man knew all about her unpaid electricity bill. He probably suspected lack of money was the reason her car ran out of petrol. That stung, because it wasn't true. Gwen raised her chin and looked him straight in the eye. 'I always pay my debts. It's finding the time to do it that's the problem.'

He nodded. 'That's why my idea is your perfect solution.' Looking closely at her face, he ran his gaze over her again and again as he catalogued all the details. 'I can see how heavily the responsibility weighs on you. When was the last time you had a decent night's sleep?'

Gwen blushed. Etienne's eyes, which until then had been riveted on her, flicked away. It was his turn to make a correction. '*Uninterrupted* sleep, that is?'

'I can't remember. There's always something that needs attention. Or somebody,' she finished lightly.

'Then why don't you look upon my offer as a way to buy yourself some time? My investment in Le Rossignol would fund extra staff, new equipment, IT training and anything else you need to make your business run more smoothly. Notice how I used the term investment. I didn't call it my *money*. I know how you feel about offers of personal generosity.' He looked at her acutely from beneath his fine dark brows.

Gwen did not share his quiet amusement. She winced

at the memory of what had happened over breakfast the previous day. Etienne didn't let that stop him for a minute. He was already moving on.

'Under this scheme, you'll be free to concentrate on the things you do best—catering and entertaining. I'd be your sleeping partner, an arrangement that will benefit us both. A *business* arrangement, that's it,' he stressed again.

Gwen hardly needed his emphasis. The perfectly produced business plan in front of her and his quiet formality would have been reassurance enough. The fact she was indeed desperate added another good hard shove in the direction of accepting his offer.

She sat on her hands. Every instinct told her to play it cool; this just seemed too good to be true. Could anyone be so kind without an ulterior motive? She organised her face into an expression of deep scepticism. It was either that, or throw herself across the desk, showering him with grateful kisses while she searched for his chequebook. She let her dangerously dishonest expression slide across the table and onto her lap. There she studied her hands with their crossed fingers, and hoped.

'I still don't know…' She squeezed the words out as though they were taxable. 'I need to think about it.'

Well—I never knew I could lie like that! she thought, astonished. In a few short hours Etienne had introduced her to all sorts of new experiences. She despised dishonesty, both in herself and others. The only way she managed to get the words out was by telling herself she wasn't actually altering the truth. She was only backing away from it.

To her surprise, the reply pleased him.

'Good—I'm glad you want to give it such careful consideration. That shows sound business sense. Study the papers, and the draft contract, too.' With a small smile, he nodded and handed her a second file from his pile of paperwork. 'And now, you have a choice. I have an appointment on the mainland, so I'm flying straight back. You can either travel with me, when you can spend a few hours wandering around the shops until I'm ready to return. Alternatively, you can stay here and enjoy what *The Windflower* has to offer while you study the paperwork at your leisure. Then, if you have any questions, we can discuss it over dinner.'

CHAPTER SIX

ETIENNE might have proved he had the selective memory of a gentleman, but Gwen was still uncertain.

'Dinner? Where? Le Rossignol isn't open tonight, and I was only going to have salad at home—'

Etienne shook his head with a smile.

'It will be served here on *The Windflower*.'

Gwen looked around, almost breathless with delight. Dinner on his private yacht sounded like heaven. It only took her a few seconds to discover the flaw in his plan.

'What happens if I haven't come to a decision by this evening?'

'It doesn't matter. I expect you'll get a certain amount of pleasure from a gourmet meal you haven't had to plan and organise yourself?' He grinned. 'I don't employ a huge staff purely for my own benefit. When I entertain a prospective business partner, I *entertain*.' He stressed his final words as though the phrase should be inscribed in block capitals over the entrance to every room. Gwen smiled, recognising again their mutual desire to put on a good show for the benefit of others. All the fight flowed out of her in an instant.

'I'd be delighted to stay here,' she said with real feeling. 'Although I'm afraid I don't have anything to wear.'

He laughed. 'If that troubles you so much, I could send someone to the *gite* to collect something for you?'

Gwen bit her lip. Her only formal dress he had already seen. Not, she reminded herself sternly, that this mattered. Her aim was to dress appropriately, not to impress him... *Yeah, right*, said the annoyingly honest voice in her head. She *could* take up his offer of a lift back to the mainland and hit the shops instead, but she didn't want to. For one thing, she couldn't afford to splash out on a new dress. For another, she was itching to sample what life on *The Windflower* had to offer. While Etienne was on shore, she could indulge her fantasies in safety. She swallowed her pride.

'My blue dress is in the wardrobe at home...'

Etienne held out his hand for her keys and Gwen handed them over in silent amazement at this man who seemed able to solve any problem and persuade her into anything. As she told him where to find all the things she would need to get ready for dinner that evening she marvelled at how helpful he was being. His reaction when he'd mentioned the name 'Angela Webbington' had disturbed her. He had presented himself then as some sort of hollow, disappointed man. Right now, nothing could look less like the truth. Etienne was his usual, charming, irritatingly compelling self. Her curiosity was well and truly aroused. What sort of grim secret could such a man be hiding? She had noticed that laptop computers were available for use in all the public areas of the ship. The temptation to find out the worst about him began to dangle before her. If Etienne assumed his past was common knowledge, he wasn't likely to care if one more person found out about it. *And putting a couple of names into a search engine hardly amounts to snooping, does it?* she reassured herself.

After pocketing her keys, Etienne reached out and patted her unexpectedly on the arm.

'My people will be very careful. You don't need to worry about a thing,' he said as his touch dropped away from her.

Gwen thought of the moment she had tried to slip out of bed and he had drawn her back into his body with those same, strong hands. Memory snatched the breath from her throat. She looked up quickly to see if he had noticed. He was looking at her, but his expression was as impassive as it had been when he was annotating his business proposition. With an awful pang she realised their moments together had passed. Any fear she might have felt at being alone with him dissolved. He wanted her business as a project now, not her body for his plaything. She had lost her chance. The only thing she had left was her dignity, and she wasn't going to let that go without a struggle. She tried to make it sound as though she were still in two minds about accepting his invitation.

'OK, thanks. What time is dinner, and where will it be served?'

'I haven't decided on either yet,' he said affably. 'Don't worry. When it's ready, I'll send a steward to find you.'

'I'm sorry I misjudged you, Etienne. You really did invite me here for business, after all!' Gwen said, trying to keep her voice light and casual.

'How could you ever doubt me?' He gave her a particularly winning smile as he escorted her to the door. 'You made it quite clear yesterday that you don't want to become my mistress. Nothing else was on offer. I'm a straight-talking man. Unlike some people, I don't make promises I can't keep.'

'I'm glad to hear it.' Gwen tried to leave it at that, but some devilish impulse forced her to add, 'It doesn't stop you keeping plenty of company, though! I lost count of how many women I saw you talking to at the reception.'

'None of them matter.' He sliced the remark at her sharply.

Taken aback by his bitter tone, she thought of his bathroom back at the chateau, stocked with cosmetics for every taste and occasion. Evidently, plenty of women passed through his hands, but none made much of an impression on him. That made his mention of the shadowy figure of Angela Webbington all the more interesting. She had mattered. Gwen's curiosity increased until she could hardly stand it.

'You're looking thoughtful, Gwen?'

She jumped guiltily, and said the first thing that came into her head. 'Do your staff treat all your female visitors the same?'

'Gwen, you are very worried about the staff. They are not here to judge you, they are here because they have jobs to do.'

He started walking away and then stopped a little short of the boardroom door. 'And of course,' he continued with a hint of mischief in his eyes, 'there's all the difference in the world between the way I introduced you as "Miss Gwen Williams" today—' standing a little apart from her, he extended his palm to an imaginary member of staff exactly as he had done earlier, up on deck '—and this…'

Before Gwen realised what was happening he had closed the gap between them and slid his arm around her waist. It enclosed her with a memory of those sublime moments they had shared as he lowered his voice to say, 'Meet Gwen, everybody…'

Instinctively, she relaxed against the delicious pressure of his arm. Almost at once it slipped away from her, like a dream. It was a painful reawakening. Gwen blinked quickly, trying to dismiss the sinful feelings that kept creeping up on her. When Etienne leaned across her in the helicopter, and now as he demonstrated his technique with conquests, the urge to take matters on her own lips and kiss him almost made a fool of her. Gwen knew she must forget their night of passion. Etienne certainly had. From the way he casually left her side and opened the boardroom door to usher her out now, he couldn't have meant anything by it. All his little gestures, like those smiles that made her feel like the only girl in the world, must be totally unconscious.

He summoned a steward to show Gwen to her suite. She swept past Etienne with what she hoped was an air of professional detachment and followed the man to her temporary home. Only then, behind locked doors, could she allow herself to grieve for what might have been.

* * *

Etienne could not watch her walk away. He went back into the boardroom, locked the door and leaned back against it. Anyone would have to break through four inches of solid mahogany and his iron determination to get in. This whole situation was bizarre. Gwen Williams was a real challenge. She confronted him with both the easiest and the most difficult situations. Here was a woman who didn't want to become his mistress. If that wasn't unbelievable enough, it really mattered to him! She was so totally unlike any other woman he had bedded. He couldn't let the memory go. They talked together then, and they were still talking now. She said things he found worth listening to. He found he wanted to know what she was going to say next. Whenever he closed a door on her, it could never quite shut her out of his mind.

It had to be because she had resisted him. That was surely the top and bottom of it. He wanted her to want him, body and soul. Anything less was unnatural. Gwen's body language kept saying yes. Yet she had refused him twice, and nothing on earth would persuade him to risk asking her again. Instead, he had changed tack and was offering her the only thing more powerful than his attraction for the opposite sex—money. It was incomprehensible that any woman would take advantage of that before his body, but Etienne had to give her the chance. Once again, she flew in the face of reason. She hadn't accepted straight away. He tried to persuade himself this was a good thing. Gwen was the first girl who had touched his heart since Angela. And, if he put her on a similar pedestal he would expect her to fall to earth with an equally leaden thud, but it hadn't happened yet, despite her circumstances.

Until he took her home and found the place was condemned to darkness, Etienne had had no idea that she was in such financial difficulty. It didn't take much imagination to realise other parts of Gwen's lifestyle would be under threat. She was obviously desperate for money, but she still held out against him. She refused to take the easy way out. He had never before known a woman with such an independent streak.

Smiling to himself, he moved away from the door. He strolled back to the boardroom table. His personal copy of her file lay on top of his pile of paperwork. Placing one long golden finger on her name, he traced over the letters.

This girl was one in a million. She fully deserved to succeed.

A steward showed Gwen to her suite. It was magnificent, with a view across gentle blue waters to the coastline beyond. He gave her an amazing guided tour of the staterooms and their private spa, but Gwen couldn't take in much detail after the first few seconds. She was more interested in the laptop on the table in her reception room. Once she was alone, she locked the door. It only took seconds to enter the name 'Angela Webbington' into a search engine.

What she discovered about Etienne's past made her wish she hadn't been in such a hurry to pry. There were pages of photographs of his ex-fiancée. Angela Webbington turned out to be a tall, whippet-thin blonde.

Gwen was built for comfort rather than speed, and cringed. Each time she looked at Etienne, she thought of sex. When he looked at her, she had a horrible feeling all he now thought was 'chef'. If this Angela was his ideal woman, then Gwen's fantasies of being leapt on again with a cry of undying lust were sadly misplaced.

She sighed. It had been a mistake to ever emerge from her kitchens. She was at her best when she was being brilliant behind the scenes. Angela Webbington was a force in front of Stateside TV cameras. *I'm fooling myself to think the other night was anything more than an accident of lust,* she thought. *I happened to be in the right place at the right time, that's all.*

She scrolled down the web page sadly, but things suddenly got a whole lot worse. A terrifying headline screamed: *'Baby or Bastard?'*, adding in only slightly smaller letters: *'"I'll disown you both!" vows future count.'* It was accompanied by a photograph of a gaunt Angela. She had been snapped leaving what the report identified as an abortion clinic. Gwen switched off the screen.

For a long time, she sat staring into space. The blank computer mirrored her thoughts. The report was simple and straightforward, but her reaction to it was complex. Etienne had been a spectacular lover, but she could not imagine him as a father. He was too much like her own dad. They were both totally absorbed by their own lives. Gwen had decided very early in life that real fathers should have a life outside work. In primary school, she had listened to her classmates' stories of holidays in foreign countries. The Williams family had been restricted to half-day trips. Her parents never travelled further than they could help. Everything revolved around the opening hours of their shop.

Gwen looked around her luxurious on-board suite. She could understand a rich man like Etienne not wanting to be tied down. There was something of that in her own character. Everything she did was a reaction against the restrictions of her earlier home life. Her move to France had scandalised her extended family, who all lived within a few miles of each other. That was bad enough, but the ultimatum Etienne had given to Angela Webbington went even further. A man who could abandon his fiancée and unborn child was surely capable of anything.

Although the room was warm, Gwen shivered.

She had known the charming Etienne had a ruthless streak, but she had not thought him capable of such coldness. She picked up his proposal and began to read it. At first, she could not concentrate. Haunted by that one incident in his life, she wanted to know more. Yet she was scared about what she might unearth. Her worries meant she only skimmed through the paperwork to begin with. Then a wicked idea took root in her mind, and began to grow. It was so terrible she could hardly bear to think it—but it was a truth that couldn't be denied.

Anyone cold-hearted enough to abandon their fiancée on the mere suspicion of infidelity was bound to succeed in business. When it came to the cut and thrust of business life, Gwen knew her limitations. She was hopeless. She let paperwork pile up. Dealing with bad payers and unreliable tradesmen kept her awake at night. When it came to cooking, she was a star performer. Anything else was a case of damage limitation. A ruthless man like Etienne Moreau would never stand for that. His money and network of advisors would be invaluable.

With him on her side, she could not fail.

She settled down to read the paperwork more carefully. It wasn't long before she realised what a good scheme Etienne was actually putting forward. Any worries she had about accepting his investment began to recede. He would provide a large sum of money up front, and the services of his marketing team would be available for free. That alone would have persuaded Gwen to sign up. The prospect of handing over the restaurant's promotion and website updating made her feel weak with relief. All she wanted to do was create dishes and cook. In return, Etienne was offering her an eighty-twenty split of the profits. She felt that was worth haggling over, so left the contract unsigned. Then she pushed it aside and tried to enjoy her spell aboard *The Windflower*.

That was easy, although it took some getting used to. At first she crept around like a mouse, half afraid she might wake and find it was all a dream. The suite she had been given was large and luxurious. There were lush arrangements of flowers on every horizontal surface, and all the rooms were cushioned with the exclusive silence that only thick, wall-to-wall carpeting could bring. The cupboards were packed with delights, in the same way Etienne's bathroom back at the chateau had been. Nothing was left to chance. She even found a cupboard filled with brand-new robes and swimming things in every size, for guests to use in the private spa.

Worrying about Le Rossignol was such a major part of Gwen's life it was hard to stop, but within an hour *The Windflower* had almost caressed it from her mind. The place was a delight from top to bottom. She had never enjoyed such a leisurely afternoon. *Actually,* she thought as she floated on her back in one of the shimmering, soft water pools, *I can't remember enjoying an afternoon off at all!*

She had spent her childhood studying, and her adulthood gaining skills. For the first time in her life she had the perfect excuse to do nothing for a few hours. She felt like a hamster released from its wheel. It was lovely. Every so often she stretched and sighed, simply because she had the space and time to do so. The sky had never seemed quite such an irresistible shade of blue as she enjoyed doing nothing, for once. The only thoughts in her head revolved around Etienne. She kept mulling over the things she had seen on the Internet. Newspaper coverage at the time had called him 'ruthless' over his handling of the Angela Webbington saga. There was no doubting his financial flair when she looked over his partnership proposal. But could she trust him? His smile made her feel like marshmallow. But the look on his face as he had stood on her doorstep, refusing to apologise, had hinted at something far darker beneath.

Despite the heat of the Mediterranean sun, she felt her skin go cold.

* * *

Etienne didn't intend wasting any time on the mainland. He sent his driver to collect the list of things Gwen wanted, while he called into his office. Working steadily, he soon emptied his in-tray, despite being distracted by a particularly tricky puzzle. Whenever he sealed a deal, he always presented the other party with a bottle of something sophisticated. So far, he had only dealt with business*men*. He knew Gwen would sign his agreement in the end, and wanted to make a similar gesture. The trouble was, he couldn't decide what it should be. Her furious reaction when he'd wanted to make her his mistress meant a bottle of vintage champagne was right out of the question. She would probably think he was just trying to get her drunk. His gift needed to be subtle, yet irresistible—like Gwen herself. He liked the perfume she wore already, and was in no hurry to change a winning formula. Without knowing its name, he was not about to risk buying the wrong brand.

He spent a long time with his brow ridged in thought. This task was outside the scope of a PA. Etienne wanted to do it alone, because Gwen deserved his personal touch. That was where his problem lay. Other women were easy to spoil. He had accounts with the finest chocolatiers and florists all over the world for exactly that reason. But he had dined at Le Rossignol often enough to know nothing could compete with Gwen's handmade luxuries. As she was currently staying on board *The Windflower,* the very last thing she needed right now was a bouquet of flowers. His staff always ensured there were armfuls of the things in every room. Any more, and the place would look like a funeral parlour. As Etienne walked out of his office he pulled out his mobile. Much as he hated to delegate in this case, it was time to enlist some help.

And then he glanced up, and saw the perfect solution to his problem.

It was displayed in a shop window on the other side of the road. Until that moment, he had been confident Gwen was totally unlike any other woman he had ever met. That was what made it impossible to get inside her guard. Now with a grin of triumph he remembered she *did* have one, single weakness. It hadn't registered with him at the time, but thinking back he recalled that she had let something slip only a few hours earlier.

Putting away his phone, he strode through the traffic to buy Gwen the present of her dreams.

While the deliciously feral shape of Etienne was away, mousy little Gwen was transformed. She was free to make the most of her chance to play. The longer she lingered aboard *The Windflower,* the bolder she got. Wistfully, she realised that if she hadn't snubbed his first offer, she might be swanning about this ship as Etienne's mistress. That illicit thought excited her. It coloured the rest of her afternoon. She swept along corridors, danced around the ballroom in solitary splendour and tried to imagine life as his *belle de jour.* She went up on deck and looked out towards the coast as though it were her own private kingdom. Somewhere out there, Etienne was busy with balance sheets and dry-as-dust docu-ments. She thought back to their session in the board-room. Smiling, she imagined his head bent over some tricky calculation. That endearing little crease would appear now and then between his brows as he applied his mind to some problem or another. Gwen had seen it so often over the past few days, but this afternoon there was a painful difference.

She was certain that, right now, she was the very *last* thing on his mind.

Gwen had just emerged from a long, luxurious shower when there was a knock at the door of her suite. Pulling on a silken robe, she hurried to open it. A steward stood outside in full uniform. He was delivering the things she had asked to be fetched from her house, but that wasn't what caught her eye. The man was also carrying a large white cardboard box, tied up with wide pink ribbon. Thanking him, she took the parcel inside her suite, wondering what on earth it could be. There was an envelope tucked inside, lying on layers of pink tissue paper. It was a card written in Etienne's distinctive handwriting. All it said was:

I saw this, and thought of you.

Gwen peeled back whisper-thin sheets of pastel paper like the petals of a rose. At their heart lay the most beautiful dress she had ever seen.

It was the full magnolia—a soft profusion of raw silk, simple, clinging and unutterably stunning. Spellbound, she lifted it up. The low-cut, subtly embroidered bodice would accentuate her voluptuous shape perfectly. The skirt fell in sensuous rustling folds to the floor. She inhaled the fragrance of luxury, long and lovingly.

And then she let slip a little moan of dismay. This was every woman's fantasy brought to life, but she couldn't possibly let it be hers. After she spent the afternoon strutting around *The Windflower* imagining life as Etienne's mistress, he presented her with this. This dress was exactly the sort of thing a man would buy his mistress. In an instant, she realised what had happened. Etienne hadn't taken her first two refusals seriously. A gift like this was a very obvious sign that he was choosing to ignore them. He assumed that because she was considering his business proposal, she would cave in to all his other demands, too. And as she imagined the silk of that dress against her skin she couldn't be at all certain that he wasn't right.

She dropped the dress as though it were suddenly red-hot. Putting her hands to her mouth, she stared around her sumptuous suite. *Appearance is everything here,* she thought. *If I wear this dress tonight, I'll fit in perfectly. And Etienne will know he's won…*

It took her a long time to get ready for dinner. As she added a dash of perfume behind her ears another knock came at the door. It might as well have been a hammer blow.

'Come in!' she called, expecting a steward who would escort her to dinner.

'I can't. I don't have a key.'

Etienne's voice came as a shock. Jumping up from her seat at the dressing table, Gwen crossed her changing room, but couldn't quite make it all the way. Memories of his ruthless treatment of Angela Webbington stopped her. She already knew sparks would fly tonight, but nothing had prepared her for the way she would feel as the showdown began.

'The door isn't locked,' she told him, in as reasonable a voice as she could manage.

When he didn't enter straight away, she walked hesitantly through her suite. Assuming the catch must have stuck, she intended to help. When the door popped open as she reached it, she jumped back in alarm.

Etienne was looking magnificent in full evening dress. His stark white cuffs were enlivened by gold studs, which he was twisting between his fingers.

'I didn't mean to startle you—' He began with a smile, and then stopped. Looking her up and down appreciatively, he studied every facet of her appearance. Then he widened his smile. 'You look lovely, Gwen. I'll get one of the seamstresses to alter the new dress for you. I'm sorry it didn't fit.'

Gwen had been primed to expect instant fury when he saw her in the blue velvet gown of their first meeting. His actual reaction completely foxed her. She reacted in the only way she knew.

'It didn't fit with my lifestyle—or the image I have of myself,' she said smartly. Picking up her handbag from a side table, she headed out into the corridor. 'Thank you for the gift, Etienne, but I've told you before. I'm here to consider your business proposal, and nothing more.'

'I know. That's why I bought you that dress. It was simply a present to celebrate our business partnership,' he said with a faint air of puzzlement. 'Whenever I enter into a new working relationship, I like to make a significant gesture. A dress seemed more your style than a gold fountain pen. Especially as you seemed sad about not having something to wear.'

Gwen hesitated, one hand lingering on the door of her suite. When he put it like that, he sounded almost convincing.

'It is a truly beautiful dress…' she agreed.

It would have been the easiest thing in the world to go back and change. But when she looked into the depths of Etienne's eyes they were dark with significance, and she knew she had been right. 'But a pen *would* have been more practical,' she added.

He lowered his head in grave acknowledgement. 'Yes, it would. I know—but I'm afraid I wasn't feeling very practical when I spotted that dress in the designer's window. Not that it matters.' He brightened, gallantly offering her his arm. 'You look absolutely wonderful.'

It was hardly the response Gwen expected, and she blushed. 'I was afraid you'd hit the roof. I thought you'd be furious,' she murmured.

'I've told you, Gwen. I don't waste words—or emotions.'

He smiled, and his expression backed him up. Gwen tried to take his arm in the spirit in which he offered it. The feel of his sleeve beneath her fingers was wonderfully provocative. She could only wonder how much more responsive she would have felt in that beautiful new gown.

Etienne looked every inch the suave, sophisticated aristocrat. Gwen had thought it was impossible for him to look better than he did the moment she first laid eyes on him. She was wrong. His perfect tuxedo, brilliant white shirt and black tie were perfectly set off by a small white rosebud in his buttonhole. His appearance almost made her forget the Internet coverage of his ill-fated affair with Angela Webbington. The tabloids had hacked out a flinty picture, but tonight there was no trace of the short-tempered, humourless man they described. Gwen hoped that pitiless nature had been exaggerated. After all, tabloids were hardly famed for being overly concerned with factual detail and as long as he confined his bad temper to her business enemies, it could be turned to her advantage. All she had to do was make sure she didn't get her own fingers burned. Or her heart.

She tried to laugh. *Chance would be a fine thing!* she thought.

Etienne frowned.

'This is a serious occasion, Gwen. It's a special dinner in honour of our new business venture.'

'Of course,' she responded quietly, thinking, *It's no wonder poor Angela disappointed him. Who could live up to standards like his?* 'You look wonderful, by the way.'

'And you look as spectacular as the moment I first saw you,' Etienne replied.

Seared by his gaze, Gwen paused. 'That's a matter of opinion!' She suddenly didn't feel very glamorous in her old dress. So she pushed on, refusing to let her feelings show. 'I should warn you that flattery is even less likely to cloud my judgement than buying me things. In any case, what makes you so sure I've decide to let you buy into Le Rossignol?' she added impishly.

He looked at her as though he could hardly believe what he was hearing.

'Only a fool would refuse such an offer, and you're very far from that,' he said, in a voice that would have cut diamond.

Gwen shot back, 'Or the size of your ego has overshadowed any thoughts of failure.'

He treated her to a smile filled with feline satisfaction. 'I've never met a woman who's complained.'

As he spoke his eyes travelled from the crown of her head down to the tips of her toes. Then his scrutiny moved slowly back up again. 'You don't need designer dresses to make you look wonderful,' he murmured. 'You have a natural beauty beyond fashion.'

'I'll bet you say that to all the girls.' Gwen chuckled, before his gaze silenced her. It was filled with the predatory tension that had thrilled her from their first meeting.

'I mean it, Gwen. Any man would be proud to escort you into dinner. I'm glad that honour falls to me this evening.' He gave a little bow. Gwen felt herself grow several inches in stature.

'The honour is all mine,' she breathed with a sparkling smile.

This was rapidly turning back into the dream to end all dreams. Etienne was so darkly handsome, and he was standing so close her heart bounced with anticipation. It took a huge effort to remember what had happened to his ex-fiancée. She had been the media's idea of a trophy partner, yet it had ended in disaster.

'Although that's as far as it's going to go tonight, Etienne,' Gwen warned quickly.

'I rather got that impression. Although it's early yet,' he added, a half-smile dancing around his lips. 'Who knows what might happen?'

Summoning up all her will power, Gwen regarded him boldly. 'I do—and it's going to be absolutely *nothing*.' She gave him a meaningfully honest smile. 'So, to get me into the mood and you out of it, how about telling me what happens to your conquests who *aren't* entirely satisfied, Etienne?'

'There haven't been any,' he said innocently as they strolled along the wide, thickly carpeted corridor towards the state dining room. Gwen hesitated. He was lying. He must be. She had seen the coverage of his broken romance, Angela the wronged fiancée and his hideous ultimatum.

'I'll prove it to you again, if you like.' He turned a slow, devastating smile on her. She pulled her hand from the crook of his arm, mostly to stop herself from leaning into him. In response he stopped and narrowed his eyes in disapproval. 'Any time, Gwen.'

CHAPTER SEVEN

LOOKING him directly in the eyes, Gwen laid her hand on his arm again. He smiled as her fingertips connected with his. It was the worst thing he could have done. Her body began to betray her with a long slow-burning blush of anticipation.

'That's better. You may not know how to accept a compliment about your appearance gracefully, but you can't possibly object to taking my arm.'

'I'm sorry,' Gwen said, and then decided to draw another line in the sand straight away. 'The truth is, I'm not used to getting praise for the way I look. It's what I do that has always mattered, to me and to others.'

'OK,' he allowed as they reached their destination. 'But I wish you had felt able to accept my gift in the innocent spirit in which it was offered. I always like to make a little gesture to my new business associates. That dress was yours.'

He stood aside to let her enter the dining room. Gwen gasped. Its walls were mirrored from floor to ceiling. They reflected a beautiful table, set with silverware and fresh flowers, a handsome man in a tuxedo—and a beautiful woman with a glow in her eyes that Gwen didn't recognise. It was a seductive picture and for the second time that day Gwen let out a little moan of dismay. Etienne strolled past her and picked something up from a place setting on the grand dining table.

'As far as I'm concerned, all you need now is this single finishing touch.'

He turned, his hands moving towards her breast. She jumped back before noticing the corsage of miniature orchid blossoms held in his fingers.

'May I?'

'Of course,' Gwen said, breathless and annoyed at herself for being so. When his warm fingers slipped between her skin and the fabric of her dress, she had a different reason to feel embarrassed. Etienne's deft movements as he secured the flowers sent a torrent of hormones surging through her body. The nearness of him and his touch was enough to turn her legs to jelly. Her discomposure was so obvious, she waited for him to comment on the effect he was having on her. There could be no denying it. Any concern she might feel for Angela Webbington now was overwhelmed by a fierce flush of arousal. She raised her eyes to Etienne's face. It was impassive.

He finished fastening her corsage and took a step back, but did not look down to admire the finished effect.

'There. That looks almost as beautiful as the wearer.'

'How can you tell? You aren't looking at it.'

'I've seen enough.'

He sauntered off to pull out her chair. When she was seated, he took the delicate linen and lace napkin from her plate. Shaking it out, he draped it over her lap. As he did so his fingers trailed across her thighs. Gwen looked up, but he was already heading for his seat on the other side of the table.

With silent efficiency, uniformed staff delivered soup and crisp rolls, warm from the oven.

'So—what is your verdict?'

Gwen was lifting a pure white curl of butter from a crystal dish set in crushed ice. Leaning forward, his dinner forgotten, Etienne looked as driven as he had done earlier in the day when he was talking business.

'It's delicious, Etienne. My compliments to your chefs. This consommé is as good as anything we serve at Le Rossignol.'

'I'm talking about my business proposition.'

That explained the tension obvious in every inch of his body. Gwen smiled and took her time coaxing the chilled butter onto her bread.

'I think it's an absolutely brilliant idea,' she said, when she thought he had waited long enough. 'My only reservation is the division of profits.'

With a sigh of relief he sat back and picked up his soup spoon.

'Knowing how independent you are, I thought you would kick if I refused to take anything at all.'

'That's right—which is why I want you to reverse the order. You're putting up the money and taking the risk, so it's only right you should get the higher amount.'

She heard his spoon click against the fine china of his soup dish. He had stopped moving. She looked up, and found him staring at her, shocked.

'You don't mean that?'

'Of course I do. I'd cook for nothing, me. Well, enough to cover my costs, anyway,' she conceded. 'I'm not interested in making a fortune. I'd rather work on my reputation as a chef.'

'You're joking,' he said quietly.

Gwen mirrored his expression of disbelief. 'No. Why would I joke about a thing like that? I'm happy enough in my work. As long as I've got enough to cover my bills, I'll reckon myself lucky beyond the dreams of millions.'

'You're saying you don't want my money?'

His voice was indistinct, as though the words were having difficulty making themselves heard through the stone wall of his disbelief.

'No, not at all. I need your investment to keep my business afloat. In return, I want you to be fairly rewarded for the risk you're taking by investing such a huge sum of money.'

His laughter was incredulous. 'It's no wonder you were too proud to wear your new dress. I might have guessed we have differing views with regard to money. That amount is nothing, believe me. It's a mere drop in the Med!'

Gwen paused, and fixed him with a knowing look. 'You know your trouble? You want a taste of real life a visit to my family home back in Wales would soon knock a few home truths into you!'

She had meant it as a joke. Etienne didn't laugh. Her own smile died as she saw the generous line of his lips struggle to rise in response.

'I don't doubt that. I've never had a home, only houses.'

'But you've got a family that goes back centuries!'

Gwen countered, thinking of his portrait gallery back at the chateau. 'It's a family that makes a home, and you've got more of that than most.'

He shook his head. 'I don't have any blood relatives left at all. My father was the last Moreau of his line. He was already an old man when I was born. He never made any attempt to hide the fact that if it wasn't for the family name, he would have remained childless until the day he died.'

Gwen almost dropped her spoon in horror. 'He told you that?'

Etienne shook his head. 'He didn't need to. After thirty years of being a widower, he married his house-keeper. I've never got on with Sophie, but my father knew I would consider it my duty to provide for her, as his widow. Watching them no doubt helped to give me rather a jaundiced view of relationships.'

This was getting heavy. Gwen tried to lighten the atmosphere and said brightly, 'Well, as long as you remember the "strictly business" rule, you'll have no problem with *our* relationship.' Her words had the desired effect. He laughed out loud.

'Gwen, I've never ridden a bicycle, but it must be exactly like dealing with you—a constant search for balance!'

She stared at him, unable to believe her ears. 'You've never been on a bike? How did you get around when you were a kid?'

'By car, of course. With a chauffeur,' he added quickly.

Gwen shook her head in amazement. 'That would have gone down a storm at Cwmbach Primary, I tell you.

Anyone turning up at the gates with a man to carry their satchel would've been dunked straight in the mud.'

'They tried that at my school. I floored them,' Etienne said succinctly. 'It wasn't as if I didn't want a bike, like all the other boys. My father finally relented when I was twelve. He presented me with the best bike money could buy, costing hundreds of thousands of francs. It came complete with more safety equipment than anyone could ever need—*including stabilisers*.' He finished in a way that told Gwen the horror of that moment had never entirely left him.

'I suppose your chateau on the Loire has plenty of private roads and tracks where you could have used them out of sight, to begin with?'

Etienne grimaced. 'That was too far beneath my dignity. If I couldn't have what I wanted on my terms, I wouldn't have it at all. I made them take it back to the shop.'

Gwen stared at him. He had been a wilful little monster in need of a good talking-to even then.

'That was a bit childish, wasn't it? Denying yourself something you really wanted, for the silliest little reason?'

'I was a child at the time. I'd never do a thing like that now,' he assured her.

'Nor me. If anybody gave me a fantastic present like that, I'd be falling all over them,' Gwen said, then fell suddenly silent. If that were true, she would be sitting there in her brand-new dress. She was as ungrateful and quick to condemn as the young Etienne had been. She looked up, expecting to feel the heat of his superiority. If he was aware of the irony of the situation, he hid it well. After checking to see that she had finished her soup, he summoned his staff. As they materialised to clear the first course Gwen came to a decision. Standing up, she cleared her throat uncomfortably.

'Would you excuse me, Etienne? There's something I have to do. I won't be a moment.'

Taking advantage of the short delay while the staff served the main course, she walked with great dignity as far as the corridor. Once out of sight, she sprinted to her suite. In seconds, she tore off her blue gown and wriggled into the spectacular silk dress. Retrieving the corsage Etienne had given her so carefully, she got back to the dining room as fast as she could. Pausing to collect herself outside the door, she took a deep breath.

The enormous dining room was echoing to the quiet efficiency of Etienne's staff. They were still plating the *Assiette de cochon de lait rôti,* but as Gwen entered everything stopped. For a fraction of a second she had the full attention of every single person in the room. Everyone stared. Then Etienne cleared his throat, and the waiters and waitresses remembered their manners. Heads down, they hurried back to work. Gwen blushed. Her shy smile was repeated on every mirrored surface, trapping her in embarrassment.

Quietly, Etienne got to his feet. Ignoring his staff, he walked straight to her side and took her arm again.

'I knew this dress was the perfect choice for you. It looks every bit as spectacular as I imagined,' he murmured warmly, gazing down at her for long moments before escorting her back to her seat.

'It feels absolutely wonderful,' Gwen agreed, twirling the orchid corsage between her fingers.

'Would you like me to fasten it for you again?' He smiled.

Her insides turned to cream and honey. This time she didn't flinch as he moved in close to her. Instead, she was disappointed when he slipped his fingers inside the shoulder of her dress to fix the flowers in a totally uncontroversial position.

From that moment on, something changed between them. Etienne relaxed in her company in a way he had not done before. They discussed the small print of the partnership contract. He called for champagne to toast their new enterprise, and Gwen's spirits bubbled like the wine. The thought of having the freedom to concentrate on her cooking while specialists did all the jobs she hated set her spirits free. Etienne was such good company, the end of their meal came far too soon. His stiff formality had given way several times, prompting Gwen to make a spontaneous offer as they finished the last mouthfuls of *Soufflé aux framboise*.

'Why don't we take coffee in my suite instead of here, Etienne? We can alter both copies of our contract at the same time,' she suggested as the waiter brought them a trolley loaded with silverware and petits fours. He considered this, then checked his watch and shook his head.

'I'm sorry. Once I've seen you safely back to the mainland, I have another appointment.'

'Oh.' She could not keep the disappointment from her voice, and he laughed.

'You're trying to knock me off balance again,

Gwen! You were so keen to stop me propositioning you earlier on! How can you have the nerve to sound disappointed now?'

'This evening has been one of the best times I've had in my life,' she said with a smile that could only hint at the strength of her true feelings. Etienne stood up. Strolling around the table, he waited while she got up from her chair. This time he did not offer her his arm.

'Surely the best time was when we were in bed together, in my chateau,' he said softly.

She held her breath, but the moment did not last. He rebounded with a chuckle. 'But that was in the past! Now we are partners in business, not crime, Gwen.'

Leaning forward, he kissed her softly on the forehead.

It was the closest she would get to his heart.

For several weeks, Gwen managed to keep up her relentless approach to work. She spent practically every waking moment at the restaurant. The pressure on her should have eased, but she was still convinced that the place couldn't function without her. Then she began to see Etienne's investment paying dividends. Instead of employing just anyone, she could afford to advertise in trade magazines for top graduates. With Etienne's advisors taking the routine work off her hands, she could spend more time in the kitchens. She experimented with new dishes to complement established favourites on the menu. Life was looking up, especially as she now had a glamorous receptionist to take over the front-of-house work she hated. There were only two tiny clouds on her horizon. One involved Etienne. He entertained at Le

Rossignol often. His fellow financiers were always men, but Gwen didn't like the way her new receptionist fawned over him. It needed a will of iron to ignore it, but her second problem had no solution at all.

Gwen now had plenty of free time, and most of it was stress-free. But no matter how much extra sleep she got, she felt permanently exhausted. That was bad enough. When she started to feel sick as well, the challenge of getting out of bed each morning became harder by the day. She hadn't taken a day off for illness since her college days, and wasn't about to start now. Some days were easier than others. As long as she kept busy, Gwen could hide the way she was feeling.

And then her period didn't arrive. That was unusual, but she managed to put it to the back of her mind. After all, she had lost weight. Telling herself that the time to worry was when the weight started piling on did not work for long. She began to worry. Etienne had taken precautions. She was sure of that. In fact, she was absolutely positive, which only made her worry more. Perhaps she was ill, not pregnant. That thought really scared her, so she worked ten times harder at the restaurant. Her bouts of sickness got worse. She could not face going anywhere near the food-preparation areas. Soon the restaurant itself began having a bad effect on her. She could not stand the smell of the flowers Etienne had delivered each week. Shortly after that, she began to feel strange all the time. Grasping at straws, she wondered if it could be put down to the Mediterranean sun. That seemed unlikely. She spent so much time at work, she was practically nocturnal. For some time, no one guessed she wasn't feeling her best. But she was fooling herself, as well as everyone else.

Gwen was piping meringue one day when she noticed her expensive new receptionist was getting agitated. The poor girl had the telephone to her ear, but wasn't able to get a word in edgeways. From the way she kept jerking it away from her head, it was a roasting, too. Putting on her best professional smile, Gwen swept out into the restaurant and lifted the receiver from the girl's hand.

'Good morning!' she announced briskly, before recognising the furious voice on the other end of the line. 'Etienne?'

He stopped in mid-rant. All trace of anger evaporated from his voice and she heard that deep, irresistible drawl.

'*Bonjour,* Gwen!'

There was genuine pleasure in her smile at the sound of his voice, and her voice reflected it. 'What can I do for you that my receptionist can't?'

'I rang to book my usual table. I will be arriving in ten minutes.'

Gwen looked around the crowded restaurant. 'I'm sorry. Absolutely every seat is taken.'

'Including the one you always keep in reserve?'

She laughed. 'Including that one! The Duke of Prestatyn brought along a couple of extra guests, so we had to do some quick rearrangements.'

Etienne chuckled indulgently. 'Archie? Don't worry about him. He's some sort of relative on my mother's side. That'll be fine. He won't mind sharing a table with me.'

'I'm sorry, Etienne, His Grace already has six people

seated around a table designed to take four. They're taking turns to breathe.'

'That's what I like to hear.' She could almost feel the warmth of his satisfaction. 'Business is booming!'

'Thanks to you. I would never have survived without your help, Etienne,' she admitted quietly.

'Yes, you would. You have all the qualities needed for success, Gwen. I merely developed your potential— in all sorts of areas.'

Gwen felt herself blushing.

'You'll never know how grateful I am, Etienne.'

'I'm sure something can be arranged!'

There was that slight chuckle in the back of his throat again. It still affected Gwen as easily and completely as ever. Heat rushed through her. She was glad this conversation was going on over the telephone. One pass of Etienne's rapier glance over her body would have told him all he needed to know. The slight flush to her cheeks and her dilated pupils would only encourage him. If he got close enough, he might just be able to hear the pounding of her heart.

She gave a little cough and tried to shake her thoughts back into some sort of order. 'Yes, I'm sure it can, but I'm afraid it won't include a table here today, Etienne. We're fully booked all the way through until closing time tonight.'

He clicked his tongue. 'I enjoy solitude, but I eat here alone at the chateau too often for it to be any sort of treat. Send me up a selection of the dishes you have on offer. Bring them yourself, and we can talk while we eat.'

Gwen's laughter diluted his heavy hint of seduction.

'I can't take time off from the kitchens when we're so busy! I'll have something ready by the time you've sent a car down from the chateau. But don't tell your friends. This isn't a takeaway. It's a special service for my very own business angel.'

'You're too kind,' he said in honeyed tones. 'But I can imagine what my chefs would say if I allowed you to do that. For you to bring me some titbits made with your own beautiful hands would be one thing. To send out for them would be disastrous. My staff would think I was heading down the trail leading to dial-a-pizza and popcorn in front of the flat screen. I would have a riot on my hands. They would abandon me. I'd be forced to exist on fast food and fizzy soft drinks.'

Gwen gave up and laughed. 'Fine, then. Even I can't condemn you to such a fate.'

'Good. Then I shall see you for lunch at the restaurant in a few minutes.'

'You'll have to sit at the table in my office, mind. It's the only place I can fit you in!' For a few seconds Gwen laughed with an ease she hadn't felt for weeks. Talking with Etienne always made everything all right again.

'That doesn't worry me at all. The satisfaction of walking through a packed restaurant will make up for having to eat in the office!' He joked so warmly it almost took Gwen's mind off her sudden, unexpected swell of nausea…

Etienne was still smiling as he reached the restaurant, a few minutes later. He had been furious at the news that there would be no table waiting for him. Then Gwen had come on the line and he remembered switching into seduction mode automatically when he first heard her. But, for the first time in his life, it had not worked immediately. Gwen had laughed and humoured him, but she hadn't giggled like a schoolgirl. She had kept a firm grip on the situation. In Etienne's experience, women rarely objected to charm and the chance to stop what they were doing to talk to him. Gwen certainly did make him work a little harder and, to his surprise, he thoroughly enjoyed it! She was playing hard to get and he'd heard it mentioned that a pleasure postponed was always sweeter. This was going to be a lunch to remember.

It was just as well he didn't realise exactly how memorable it would turn out to be.

As Etienne strode into the restaurant his smile soon faded. Greetings and waves were ignored as he scanned the packed tables. Gwen was nowhere to be seen. It was one of her inflexible rules that no guest was left to linger in the reception area. Within seconds the new receptionist appeared and directed him towards the bar.

'Where is *Mademoiselle le chef*?'

'I'm afraid she's indisposed at the moment, *monsieur*. Can I help you?'

'Gwen is arranging a table for me in her office,' he said smoothly, as the girl looked in need of an explanation.

'That might be rather difficult, *monsieur*. Her office is in use at the moment. I'll get you a drink.'

Etienne ordered a martini he didn't want. He scanned the crowd, looking for Gwen's beautiful face and listening for her laughter. He was getting impatient but when he looked at his watch it was to see that barely ten minutes had gone by since he arrived. It felt like several lifetimes. What was going on? She was always a professional to her fingertips, but there was no sign of her anywhere today. He took his drink over to a seat in the corner of the bar area. It gave him a good view of the whole restaurant, but not the one thing he really wanted. Running a finger idly around the rim of his glass, he waited. Time passed, but she did not appear. Unused to waiting for anything, Etienne became restless. Something must have happened. It was unthinkable for his arrangements to be delayed like this. She knew he was coming. Where was she?

He was about to walk over and rap on her office door when it was flung open wide. Gwen emerged with a smile and a quip for the nearest diners, but Etienne was not fooled for a second. Pausing only briefly to give a distracted greeting to his cousin the duke, he moved quickly across the room to her side.

'Gwen? What is it?'

'Etienne! I hope we haven't kept you waiting!'

'That doesn't matter. It's you I'm worried about. You look terrible.' His gaze sharpened. 'What's the matter?'

'Nothing. I'm fine. It's all perfectly under control.'

She turned to walk away. He grabbed her arm to stop her, but used a little too much force. She yelped, causing him to release his hold but it was too late. Everyone within earshot looked up.

'I'm sorry, I trod on *mademoiselle's* toe,' Etienne explained, smoothly bundling Gwen back into her office. There he slammed the door and leaned back against it.

'There's no escape until you tell me what is going on.'

'You wanted lunch here.'

She hesitated, and her features moved in a way that worried him. When she spoke again it was with an obvious effort.

'I was getting the room ready. After all, I can't expect a French count to eat off a tray, can I?' She tried to laugh, but it was no use. Looking around the office with its neatly ordered files of paperwork and pot plants, Etienne knew she had been doing nothing of the sort. There was a cold compress, a glass of iced water and a large bowl on the coffee table.

'I'm not buying that excuse. You're too pale, Gwen. And you've got such dark circles under your eyes.' Stretching out one finger, he touched her cheek experimentally. Gwen shrank away from his touch.

'You're sick, aren't you?' he persisted.

Her eyes popped in horror. 'No! Don't say that word in here! If the customers hear, they'll think it's food poisoning. I'll be closed down!'

'It isn't, is it?'

Gwen was horrified by his suggestion. 'Of course not, no! I'm scrupulous about hygiene. I eat exactly the same thing as all the rest of the staff, and no one else has suffered so much as a headache for weeks.'

Etienne watched her closely. Now he came to study her with a financier's mentality rather than the eye of lust he noticed that the curves he remembered so fondly were not quite as generous as before.

'When you can keep it down,' he suggested. 'You've lost weight, Gwen.'

'Everyone does in summer. It's the heat and all the salads. I'm fine, Etienne, really.'

He made a noise in his throat, hinting at his deep scepticism.

'OK…as long as you're sure.'

Gwen had hardly finished nodding before the most awful feeling washed over her again. She lurched for the bowl and was heartily sick. Etienne was there with words of encouragement, but his attitude changed the moment she tried to tell him it was nothing.

'It's far from nothing, Gwen. You're too ill to work. I'm going to call my doctor, and then I'm taking you home. You're not setting one foot inside this restaurant again until we've found out what this is all about.'

The fact she was too weak to argue gave him no pleasure at all. Hustling her out the back way with a quick word to the receptionist, he drove to her cottage at top speed. She was still wobbly as she got out of the car. When he tried to carry her upstairs she was well enough to put up a spirited defence.

'I don't need your help, Etienne. I'm fine and I certainly don't need you carrying me up any more stairs!'

He was affronted. 'If I wasn't a gentleman I would laugh at the suggestion that something might happen today. I would never take advantage of a sick woman.'

'I keep telling you, I'm not sick! It's nothing. It'll pass off. It always does.'

'You mean this has happened before?'

'Once or twice, maybe.' She shrugged like an insolent child.

'Really? So exactly how long has this been going on?'

'I don't know!' She pushed her curls back irritably from her forehead. 'A couple of weeks? Maybe longer. I haven't been taking notes. I'm too busy working. As I've told you before, I don't have the time to be ill.'

Etienne's personal doctor was there within minutes. He took one look at Gwen and frowned.

'We have not met before?'

'No, I'm Etienne's business partner.'

Gwen waited for the man to laugh or make some suggestive comment. Instead he smiled quite innocently before asking if there was a Mr Williams. For the first time, Gwen felt fear. She looked at Etienne with terrified eyes.

'Next of kin, you mean? Oh, my God! It's *that* serious?'

'Not necessarily.' The doctor was quick to smile. 'If it was anyone but you who had called me in, Etienne, I'd start by asking Mademoiselle Williams the obvious question.'

'Which is?' Gwen looked from one man to the other. She was really scared now.

'I'd merely enquire if there's any way you could be pregnant, Mademoiselle Williams,' the doctor said in a matter-of-fact way. Gwen stared at him. He smiled back, his expression gently prompting.

It was the one cause Gwen flatly refused to acknowledge. She had made a million excuses to herself and tried to ignore all the signs, but this was the showdown. She felt like the *SS Titanic*, steaming towards a giant iceberg labelled disaster.

'I—I don't know.' Shocked, Gwen appealed to the doctor with her eyes. But he had turned away, preparing to take a blood sample.

'It's a question I ask all young women as a matter of

course, that's all. When they present with bouts of sickness but are otherwise fit and healthy, it's the most natural thing in the world to suspect pregnancy.'

She blinked at him, lost for words. Etienne was equally staggered.

'*What?* But I can't see how you could possibly be pregnant,' he said faintly.

'That's staff for you, Etienne.' The doctor grunted.

Gwen was appalled at his bedside manner and in other circumstances would have called him on it, but she was too shocked by the possibility of pregnancy to say anything. She looked away quickly as the blood started to flow from her arm and into the vacuum container. There was silence in the room. It was broken only by the warble of birdsong outside, floating in from the garden. The doctor wrote Gwen's name on the phial of her blood, his pen scratching through the tension. Finally Etienne walked over to the window. Hands on hips, he stared out across the valley. His voice, when it came, was as parched as the landscape.

'It's impossible. We only spent one night together.'

It was the doctor's turn to stop and stare.

'You mean you and Mademoiselle Williams…' Frowning, he turned his full attention on Gwen, aghast.

Gwen sprang up to defend herself, but Etienne was already there. Whirling away from the window, he caught her by the shoulders. The look in his sloe-dark eyes was enough to silence her.

'It can only be me. That's right, isn't it, Gwyneth?'

He called her by her full name. Gwen shuddered. She had thought she was in trouble. This confirmed it.

The doctor looked distinctly uneasy. 'That's ridiculous.'

'But why should you automatically think Etienne wasn't the father of this…' her nerve almost failed her, and she took several attempts to force the word out '…baby?'

It wasn't the doctor who answered, but Etienne himself. 'The doctor knows my views. I think a child should have two responsible parents,' he said stiffly.

It was an answer. Whether it was the whole truth, Gwen wasn't sure. She couldn't help but think about the baby Angela Webbington had aborted. Which part of that unhappy couple had been the irresponsible one?

'What can I say?' The doctor shrugged, addressing his gesture of exasperation to Etienne.

'Nothing. Don't say a thing, Doctor. If Gwyneth is pregnant, then she and I will sort this out together, between us.'

His smooth reply sounded almost practised. The icy calm was certainly enough to freeze Gwen's blood. Alerted to the possibility she might be carrying Etienne's child, the doctor carried out the rest of his examination with that in mind. All the signs were there, he told them, but official confirmation would have to wait.

'That's fine. You have the number of my mobile. Ring the moment you know. I'll deal with everything here,' Etienne said, hustling the doctor out of the room.

A cold knot of dread tightened inside Gwen. She had a horrible suspicion she knew exactly what he meant.

She sat on the edge of her bed, staring at the floor. Her hands were clasped so tightly together the knuckles ached. She heard Etienne and the doctor muttering outside her window. She couldn't hear what they were saying, and didn't care. Her whole life had stuttered to a halt. From now on she would have to exist at second hand. All her time and energy would have to be devoted to the little life growing inside her. She could feel motherhood closing in on her like the walls of her room.

Several centuries later, she heard a car drive away. It was only one car, and it lacked the high-class purr of Etienne's pulling machine. She waited, expecting him to leave too. Instead, she heard slow, heavy footsteps come up the stairs. He was coming back. She braced herself for a confrontation. It was only a matter of feet across the landing to her bedroom. Gwen did not move as she sensed Etienne reach her threshold. There was no point. He would have a face like thunder, and the smallest movement from her would unleash his fury. She tried to concentrate on the hum of bees, busy in the thyme flowers growing on the sun-drenched terrace. It was supposed to be a diversion. Instead it reminded her of the buzz of disapproval this news would provoke among all her relatives back home.

'How do you feel?'

Gwen's head jerked up before she could stop it. She had expected anger. Strained compassion was the last thing she anticipated. His expression was impassive. She knew he must have been fighting to keep his true feelings under control, exactly as she was.

'Terrible. I've ruined everything,' she muttered, dropping her gaze back to the rag rug.

She heard him take a step towards her. The room

wasn't very big, but he was still as far away from her as it was possible to be while still sharing the same space. After a pause, he took another step, and then a third. Now the tips of his leather shoes intruded into her narrow field of vision. She waited. Eventually, a shadow moved and she felt his touch. It fell lightly against her shoulder. When she did not move, he dropped its full weight on her, stiff and unyielding. She couldn't be sure if it was meant as a comforting gesture. His fingers felt like wood. *Like my heart,* she thought bleakly.

'You aren't entirely to blame, Gwen. It took two of us.'

It was an admission wrung from him like blood, she could tell.

'I must have been mad when I agreed to stay with you. I've never done anything like that before. What was I thinking of?' Her voice was an agonised whisper. The pressure of his hand released and then fell again in something that was supposed to be a reassuring pat. Gwen was beyond appreciating his efforts.

'I'm always scrupulous about...' the hand on her shoulder twitched with his discomfort '...precautions. I don't understand how this can possibly have happened—'

He spoke slowly, but Gwen's response was like quicksilver. 'You aren't trying to deny this baby is yours, are you? You can't control everything—accidents happen, Etienne.'

Pulling away his hand, Etienne looked down on her with naked scorn.

'You must believe it!' she said frantically. 'You said as much yourself, to the doctor!'

'Of course I know it's mine,' he growled. 'What do you think I am?'

'I don't know.' Gwen subsided onto the bed again. 'And I don't know what I'm going to do, either.'

At her words he moved more quickly than he had done since entering her house. Sitting down beside her, he whipped out his mobile phone.

'You don't have to do a thing. Not a single, solitary thing. This is my responsibility, so I shall take care of everything.'

Gwen's brain sprang to life. All the news reports she had seen about Angela Webbington rattled through her brain with the urgency of Etienne's fingers on his keypad. With a scream of horror she leapt away from him.

He stopped and stared at her, dismayed at her reaction. 'What is it? What have I done now?'

'Nothing. You aren't going to do anything to me!'

Gwen began to panic. Backing towards a corner, she wrapped her arms tightly around her waist. She stared at him, wild and wide-eyed. Etienne watched her. His expression hardened from alarm to pity. As it did so, he went back to tapping out a number on his phone.

'Oh, yes, I am,' he announced sharply. 'I'm going to marry you.'

CHAPTER EIGHT

GWEN was too amazed to speak. This was the last thing she had expected and she didn't know what to think. There was a moment of relief—he was not threatening her baby—but then panic loomed again as Etienne continued.

'I'm responsible for this situation. I must take the consequences, and pay my dues.'

He made it sound like a parking offence.

'You can't just announce it like that!' She gasped. 'Don't I have any say in the matter?'

'Why would you want anything different?' He stared at her, mystified. 'Our child will be the legitimate heir to the Moreau name. Some day it will inherit my title, and everything I've worked for on my own account. What could be better than that?'

'But…' his reasonable tone left her scrabbling for objections '…I'm a chef…and you're a count!'

'That will make you the perfect wife for me.' Etienne's voice was strained through centuries of breeding. 'Your work at Le Rossignol has shown me how good you are in social situations, however difficult.

You have a decent enough business brain and grace under pressure. You will make the perfect countess,' he said as if there were no question about it. He had spoken, and it would be her duty to obey.

'Have you stopped to consider for one single second that I really might not want to marry you?'

'What?' Etienne stared at her. He looked genuinely surprised. 'No. Of course I haven't.'

Gwen nodded. She should have known. What sort of a relationship was this? They knew nothing about each other beyond the confines of business. She had served him with a coffee. He had given her a lift home. She had fallen into his arms. That was just about the extent of it. They had only one thing in common. It was the whirlwind excitement of one passionate night. An hour earlier, the thought of marrying Etienne would have been an impossible fantasy—something she had not dared admit to herself. Unconsciously, her hand strayed to her stomach, curving protectively. Now the fantasy had suddenly become a cold-hearted business deal.

'What is the matter, Gwen? Why are you looking at me like that? You can't honestly be about to refuse.' His voice was gently mocking. 'I've never known a woman who wouldn't jump at the chance to become a countess.'

Gwen thought of his stepmother, the odious Sophie, and her poor, nervous niece.

'Well, you know one now,' she announced.

Etienne hit back with an equally solid response. 'This isn't about what either of us wants as individuals. This is about *my* heir, *your* pregnancy, and *our* baby. We have to stop thinking about ourselves and put all our energy into preparing for the future.'

He sounded so aristocratic, so certain. 'Our lifestyles are so different,' she said faintly. 'What about your future?'

'My future is never in any doubt. Let me handle this, Gwen.' He moved as though to put an arm around her shoulder. At the last moment, he hesitated and turned the movement into just a reassuring touch of his hand.

When it came to keeping Le Rossignol afloat, Etienne had been as good as his word. He had not interfered. Gwen wondered whether he would be content to throw money at parenthood in a similar way. She didn't know whether he would back off or take compete control. With her mind in a whirl and no idea how she would set about raising a child, she didn't know which would be worse. That alarmed her.

She searched his face, trying to see the emotions behind his dark eyes. It was so tempting to give in—simply to let him take control and sweep her away.

'I don't have a clue about babies, and there's so much to do if we're going to get married before I'm...' Instinctively, she looked down at her waist. It was still neatly defined, but for how much longer?

'That's the great thing about being a member of the aristocracy. Contingency plans for all the major life events are permanently in place. They only need a few phone calls to set them in motion. And relax—I don't know anything about babies either. I doubt if many first-time parents do. And we'll have more than enough help.'

Gwen watched him tap numbers into his phone and start mobilising his staff. He was oblivious to everything else, so she could observe him in detail. He was still the gloriously handsome, detached figure who had walked into her life on that fateful first evening. This cool professionalism had always been one of his attractions. He shared her need to be in control of every situation. With a surge of desire she saw he was determined to be a part of her baby's future. Etienne barely noticed her interest in him. He was a man in a hurry. The moment he closed his call, he picked up her handbag and set off downstairs. 'Come on. Let's discuss this on neutral territory.'

'Where are you going with my bag?'

'We're going for a drive. This is the bait to get you into my car.' He dangled her bag from his fingers as he opened the passenger door of his Ferrari for her. Gwen came to a halt on her front doorstep.

'Where are we going?'

He gave her a smile that was almost encouraging. 'There's no need to look so suspicious. I know a little bistro right out in the country. The owners are very discreet. We won't be troubled and we can talk freely. There's no risk of being overheard.'

'I'm going to have a baby. What is there left to say?' Gwen concentrated on the ground as she walked towards the car.

'We're going to be married; there are many things to discuss. And let's get one thing straight from the beginning. You're not having *a* baby. You are carrying my child. There is a difference. It means you aren't alone.'

Everything had changed, yet some things were still the same. Etienne was looking at her in the same way he had done over the conference table on *The*

Windflower. He was perfectly composed and in control. And he was still as spectacular as ever. A treacherous suspicion of hunger stirred within her, sealing her fate.

'OK. A discussion over lunch. I can handle that,' she said, trying to gain some control over her dangerous emotions. It would not be a good time to let her feelings get the better of her. She was too confused to know what they were.

Etienne's mouth tightened. 'Yes. There are things I must talk to you about.'

'In the same way you "talked" to Angela Webbington?' Gwen queried, remembering the coverage she had seen of their stormy relationship. Her accusation did not have the effect she expected. Instead of exploding with rage or denial, Etienne simply nodded.

'*Oui.* In exactly that way. Only this time, each of us is going to listen to what the other has to say, Gwen.'

She fell silent. Angela had vanished from his life. Gwen couldn't help wondering if the same thing might happen to her, if she refused to toe his line. She thought of being responsible for a tiny new baby and never seeing Etienne again. Suddenly, a fierce wave of longing engulfed her. Marrying Etienne would give her child a safe, secure life and keep them both within his orbit.

'So…if I marry you, it's a guarantee that everything will be all right?'

Staring resolutely through the windscreen, he eased his car into gear and pulled away. Unusually the Ferrari moved off with dignity, rather than in a shower of gravel.

'Not even I can promise that, Gwen. Nobody can predict what the future holds. But I can promise you one thing. We are going to do this together. My child will be raised to take his place as the next count. He is owed the best of everything, and I intend to see that he gets it, whatever that takes. My responsibility for him began the moment I got you—' he waved a hand in the general direction of her lap '—the moment all this happened. I would never abandon a woman to bring up a child of mine alone—least of all you. We're partners in business. This is a joint effort, too.' He glanced across at her with an encouraging smile.

'Did you talk to your ex-fiancée in this deeply romantic way?' Gwen sent the question spinning towards him like a guided missile. Etienne flicked it aside with a grimace.

'You are not Angela, and you never will be,' he said with such painful restraint Gwen wondered again what Angela had really been like to have had such an effect on this man. 'Things are going to be very different this time.'

Gwen had been warning herself for weeks that it was a bad idea to bring her feelings into this business partnership. Now he would be increasing his influence over her personal, as well as her professional, life. If she agreed to marry him, she might soon be unable to afford the luxury of any emotions at all.

He drove on. His silence was as arid as the countryside flashing past the car. When they stopped, Etienne took his time in going around to open the door for her. She blinked in the harsh sunlight. They were in a little village square, sleepy with heat. Luckily, there were few people around. No one would recognise her when she was this far out in the wilds, but that didn't mean she wanted people to see her at a time of total turmoil.

The bistro's proprietor rushed out, wreathed in smiles. He met them like visiting royalty. In spite of herself, Gwen's heart fluttered a little to see Etienne greeted so kindly, and by his title. Then she thought back to the Internet coverage she had seen of his past. Etienne was famous for his vast number of female 'friends'. He must have brought dozens of girls here in the past. How could marriage change a man like that?

They were led away from the public areas of the restaurant to a secluded table set beneath a bower of vines and creepers. Spectacular passion flowers studded the greenery, their pure white flowers pencilled with blue and yellow detail.

'Gwen will drink fresh orange juice over ice, she'll start with melon and strawberries, followed by the poached fish and salad. And make sure everything is well washed in Evian,' Etienne announced to the waiter.

Gwen said nothing until they were alone together.

'Don't I get any choice in my food?'

'Was there anything you particularly wanted?'

'No, but—'

'Then relax!' He tried to smile. This time his efforts were slightly more successful. 'I've simply saved you the task of choosing the healthiest options. My child will have only the best.'

Gwen heard nothing after that. She tried to listen, but it quickly became obvious Etienne's mind was made up with regard to every detail regarding her, his child, his heritage and his future. Etienne was laying out his big ideas as they applied to her baby, and life in general. Her function was to listen, and presumably nod in all the right places. Unable to think about the implications, she concentrated on her meal. Her earlier wave of sickness was a distant memory, and now she was ravenous. As it turned out, Etienne had made all the right choices for her. Her food was totally delicious. *Damn the man*, she thought mutinously.

'And what do you have to say to all this, Gwen?'

Etienne's question caught her completely off guard.

'I—I don't know. The only thing I know about motherhood is that I'm not cut out for it,' she said hopelessly. 'I've only just managed to escape one family. This taste of freedom after being suffocated for so long has been incredible. Le Rossignol is my life now. How can I sacrifice that, when I've worked so hard to get it? I've only had a few weeks to enjoy it. I've hardly begun to live. Now I'll have to spend the rest of my life running around after…somebody else.'

Etienne did not answer, but his face darkened and he summoned the bill. 'Let's get home. The doctor should have your results by the time we get there.'

Gwen let him lead her back to the car. As he held the door open for her she saw a perfect illustration of what her future might hold. It was trailing across that pretty little village square.

'Gwen—what is it?' Etienne's voice sharpened. Afraid she might be about to faint, he reached out and caught her by the shoulders. Pulling her towards him, he was ready with reassurances, but they died on his lips.

She wasn't looking at him. She was staring over his shoulder. He raked the village square with a glare, but couldn't be expected to see it in the same way she did. It was practically deserted. A few white doves pecked around the feet of some old men enjoying the afternoon in the shade of an ancient walnut tree. Meanwhile, a screaming toddler was being dragged across the cobblestones by a harassed young woman weighed down with shopping. She was struggling on alone, with no one to help her.

Gwen saw, and understood. She was alone and pregnant in a foreign country. But Etienne had helped her once before and, whatever had happened in his past, she did have complete faith in his ability to protect her and her baby. Who was she to jeopardise her child's future simply through fear for her own heart?

'It's nothing. I'm fine,' she reassured him with a wan smile. 'I just caught a glimpse of what life might be like on my own, that's all.'

'I must get you back to the chateau,' he said with concern. 'You look exhausted. It's been a hectic few weeks. You need rest—whatever the outcome of your tests.'

The doctor delivered her results in person. They were positive, as both Gwen and Etienne had known they would be.

'I shall need a full report on my...*fiancée's*—' Etienne spoke the word with difficulty '—condition, and written lists of your recommendations for her care and diet,' he began, then spent the next half an hour grilling the doctor about what would happen, minute by minute. Locked inside her own thoughts, Gwen hardly heard a word he said.

'I'm not up to this, Etienne,' she said miserably. 'I don't know how to be a mother! And what about the restaurant? I need some time to get used to all this—'

'Haven't you been listening? You don't need to do anything. From now on, I shall be taking care of absolutely everything for you.'

Gwen felt again the stirrings of unease. Her life was spinning entirely out of her control. Etienne's words tailed off, his smile fading as he saw her expression.

As he sensed that she was wavering his voice became soothing, a velvet glove encasing cold, hard steel. 'I keep telling you. This is a team effort. Between us, we're going to give our baby the best of everything.' When she did not answer, he continued, in an appeasing tone, 'You've often said how traditional your family are. I could ask your father's permission to marry you, if you like.'

Any colour Gwen might have regained disappeared as she saw Etienne pulling out his mobile. 'No! My parents must never know I got things back to front!' She was adamant. 'As you said, they're old-fashioned. It's wedding first, babies later as far as they're concerned.'

Etienne tucked his phone away again. 'Fine. Just as you like. My people will get all the paperwork sorted out. The moment it's complete, we'll marry with the minimum of fuss. Then we'll fly straight to your parents. You may not want me to ask their permission formally, but they will be the first to know. It's the least

I can do. Trust me, Gwen. Everything will be over and done with in a few signatures,' he assured her. 'My people will do everything, including the catering—for once, you will not need to lift a finger.' Gwen's head was whirling, filled with so many panicked thoughts that she could hardly muster a single straight sentence. One thought, however, was clear.

'So…I'm not going to have a hand in catering for my own wedding?' she said slowly.

Etienne looked puzzled. 'Why would you want to? It's your big day. You'll want to mingle with my friends and family. I've seen how much you enjoy the social aspect of your work at the restaurant.'

'But I hate all that, Etienne! I only do it for the sake of my business!'

'I'm not so sure, Gwen. No one could fake the way you handle yourself in a crowd, and deal with the diners. You'll be the new public face of the house of Malotte. It's about time we had an injection of brains and beauty. The Moreau family has cornered the market in fighters and philanderers for centuries. I'm going to turn our little accident into the best thing that has ever happened to my family.'

Gwen was silent for a long time. If she married Etienne, would there be any room left for her? It already felt as if she were drifting away—dwindling into someone smaller and weaker. But what were her options here? She didn't want an abortion, her family certainly had no money to spare and would be horrified by her predicament…and here was Etienne, determined to take care of everything. Was it such a high price to pay? It was his duty to do the best for his ancient family. He wanted it to do more than simply survive. He wanted it to thrive, and that was exactly what she wanted for her baby. It was an unromantic basis for a marriage, but, to use his executive-speak, it ticked all the right boxes for both of them. Not simply practical boxes either. Looking at Etienne now, she saw his eyes glowing with enthusiasm for his latest project. Unable to help herself, she thought back to the one unforgettable night they had shared. She felt the memory warm her like a caress.

'When you put it like that, who am I to refuse?' she said at last.

CHAPTER NINE

FROM that moment, Etienne would not let Gwen lift a finger or take any decisions. His staff swung into action. Within hours most of her belongings had been moved out of the *gite* and installed in the chateau. He supervised everything, including Gwen. Whenever he saw her, he complained if she wasn't sitting down, eating something nourishing or preferably doing both at once. The whole estate became a visible whirlwind of activity. Wherever Gwen went, it felt as though she was in the way. A constant procession of gardeners brought flowers into the house for the indoor staff to arrange. The building was filled with the sounds of curtains being pulled back and squadrons of cleaners opening up long-locked rooms. When the racket finally stopped and Gwen escaped to her new bedroom that evening, she fell asleep within seconds. Doing nothing was turning out to be more exhausting than working for a living.

She woke next morning into a glorious delusion. Opening her eyes to see the unfamiliar surroundings, for a few seconds she imagined Etienne must have swept her into his bed again. Then she realised she was alone. Almost straight away, a feeling of nausea threw her out of bed. It shredded her dreams with the efficiency of a *demi-lune*. Already exhausted, she dragged herself into the shower room. The surroundings of cool green marble revived her a little, and she managed to summon up enough energy to check its cupboards. Her bathroom, like Etienne's, was stocked with a staggering array of soaps, gels and moisturising milks. The whole place hummed gently with a cocktail of organic, plant-based fragrances. She settled on a bottle of invigorating shower gel allegedly chock-full of sea minerals. Ten minutes beneath a spray head the size of a dinner plate was enough to start her thinking about breakfast. In the time it took her to dress in a black skirt and simple white blouse, she was ravenous. Despite her dread of meeting anyone who might tell her to sit down or go back to bed, she set off in search of food.

The chateau was enormous, but the silence of its sunlit halls meant the smallest sound travelled for many metres. She soon found her way to a spectacular vaulted room on the ground floor, overlooking a courtyard garden.

Etienne was already seated at the head of a long dining table. When he saw her enter the room, he folded his newspaper and stood up with a smile.

'*Bonjour*, Gwen. I hope you enjoyed a restful night?' His voice was resonant with concern.

'Thank you. It was wonderful.' *But lonely*, she added to herself. She headed towards the breakfast display, set out on an enormous antique sideboard like the one she remembered from that first fateful night.

'Take a seat. The waitress will fetch anything you need.' Etienne indicated the far end of the table, remote from him. Sure enough, a woman in a severe black dress and white apron moved soundlessly into position.

'But the food is only a few yards away!' Gwen protested.

'You need to have a break, Gwen.' Etienne dismissed her protest with a shrug. 'You've been working too hard, and you are run-down and tired. That is not good for a pregnant woman. So you will be pampered for a while—enjoy it. *Both* of you.'

Far away in a distant part of Etienne's cavernous house, a mason's drill hummed into life. As she gave her order for fresh fruit salad and tea Gwen frowned, and not only at the idea of someone fetching and carrying for her over such a short distance.

'This house seems perfect to me, Etienne. Why does it have to be put under attack by builders?'

'I bought it for its position, beauty and history. It was always going to be too large for a single man, especially while I was dividing my time between so many other properties. It only makes more work for the staff, so I concentrated the restoration work on my suite and the few rooms I needed downstairs. Now you will be a permanent resident here, we shall need every inch of space. You will want to entertain,' he explained.

Gwen was not convinced. 'You said this place was your bolt hole. It's supposed to be somewhere you can escape, and get away from people.'

'Yes, but that was before you became pregnant.'

He made it sound like an accusation. She reddened angrily. 'Don't try and make out it's all my fault!'

'I'm not. There's no point in trying to apportion blame. The damage has been done, so I'm adapting to it. I can't expect you and my baby to live like hermits.'

At his direct mention of the baby, Gwen panicked. Scrabbling for a sheet anchor, she looked at her watch. 'Look at the time! I'll have to hurry if I'm going to get to Le Rossignol before the florist delivers—'

'There's no need. Relax!' Etienne said solicitously. 'You employ plenty of staff there now. Let them deal with it. If you want something to do, why don't you try a makeover of the chateau menus? I'm sure Chef would be willing to negotiate.'

Gwen pulled back as though she had been burned. She couldn't imagine a life without her work. It defined her, and gave her a purpose in life.

'That's very kind of you, Etienne, but I'd rather we stuck to our usual arrangement when it comes to the restaurant.' It was all she could do to hide the panic in her voice. '*Laissez-faire*—isn't that what it's called?'

'Why worry about the place when you don't have to?' He laughed off her concern. 'You have a new role now. I'm not going to let you out of my sight for an instant.' He was starting to look quite pleased with himself. 'We will elect a temporary manager. He can be in charge of the day-to-day running of the restaurant while you're distracted. You told me you were happy enough just to cook. Use my investment to make it easy for yourself. You need rest and supervision to make sure my heir gets the very best possible start in life.'

'Are you suggesting this because you think I can't manage?' she said slowly.

'No partner of mine should be content to merely "manage". I want you to be completely relaxed and happy, Gwen. That is an entirely different state of mind. Look at the difference our business partnership has made to you in only a few weeks. You've been freed from the treadmill, you've had time to rest, and concentrate on the part of the job you love best.' His voice dropped to an appreciative whisper. 'You are a completely different woman from the one I met all those weeks ago.'

'For better, or worse?' Gwen put her head in her hands.

Etienne shot a meaningful look at the maid. She took the hint and evaporated from the room. After a suitable silence, Gwen heard Etienne stand up and walk slowly towards her. She did not move a muscle. When he reached her end of the table, he pulled out the nearest chair. He dropped into the seat. His arms in their smart, dark business suit intruded into her line of sight. He was ready for work. She didn't feel ready for anything— especially when he reached out and gently pulled her hands away from her face. Clasping them in his, he looked deep into her eyes. Once again, she was trapped in the smouldering intensity of his gaze. He was studying her in a way that laid her feelings bare. It redirected the heat of her anger in a way that scared her. Surely, mothers weren't supposed to feel desire. They were supposed to be down-to-earth, and sensible.

'Gwen, I have made some terrible mistakes in the past.' His words were heavy with something she assumed was reassurance. 'I realise that now, and don't intend to repeat *any* of them. I won't allow you to face this alone. That's why things must be like this. My son is going to have the best possible start in life. Believe me.'

She watched him, watching her. His eyes were dark with determination, and the set of his jaw was totally resolute.

With the delicacy she remembered so well, his thumb began to draw slow shapes over the back of her hand.

'It's all in hand. Flowers, food, stationery, ceremony—the whole show is already on the road, as you say. My people have organised everything. You don't have to do a thing—except edit your part of the guest list.' He went on, oblivious to her growing horror. 'When I came into your room late last night to see if you wanted anything, I saw your address book on the bedside table. My PA put it straight onto a database.'

Gwen found herself totally unable to speak. That didn't matter. Etienne was more than happy to do that for her—along with everything else, apparently.

'You looked so peaceful—' he began with a smile, but 'peaceful' was the last thing Gwen felt. Rigid with rage and furious at the effect he continued to have on her, she wrenched her hands from his grasp.

'So you took my address book in the same way you've taken over the rest of my life?' She stood up, shaking. 'It hardly sounds like you need me at all. In fact, I might as well say goodbye to you right now, Etienne, rather than clutter up your itinerary any further!' She heard him call her name, but did not look back.

Twenty minutes later, Gwen was pacing back and

forwards in her room, going over arguments to use against him and trying to calm herself before going back down, when she heard a familiar sound. It was Etienne's car prowling along beneath her window. He was leaving for the office, without saying goodbye. The realisation sliced into her heart. For the first time, the full horror of the situation swept over her. Independence was so important to her that she had travelled halfway across Europe to find it, and ended up *pregnant* by a man who knew nothing about her—who, she now realised, saw her as nothing but a ticket to his heir.

She buried her face in her pillow, but there was no time for tears. She had made her choice. For the sake of her baby, she was determined to make the best of this. However much she might ache inside.

Efficient as ever, Etienne had already put his staff to work. Within moments, Gwen got a text from his PA. An appointment had been made for her at Malotte's most fashionable beautician. All she had to do was turn up. Everything else was in hand. Sure enough, as she was reading the text she heard one of the estate's limousines being drawn up outside the main villa doors.

She went down to tell the chauffeur she would drive herself, in her own car. It was hopeless. Etienne's system didn't allow for alterations. From now on, she would ring for a chauffeur whenever she wanted to go anywhere at all. Gwen bit her tongue, and counted to ten. She couldn't rail at the staff. It was hardly their fault if the Count of Malotte wanted to dictate her every move. Bottling up her anger, she tried to console herself.

She wouldn't have the hassle of driving through Malotte's narrow, twisting streets, or finding a parking space. There might be advantages to Etienne's guilty conscience after all.

A shame they didn't make up for the loss of her freedom.

Summer was flying away. The nightingales had already vanished from the overgrown margins of the chateau grounds. They had escaped before the chill of winter. How Gwen wished she could follow them. She gazed out of the window as the assistant put the finishing touches to her makeover. The village square was drenched in sunshine. Outside, in flickering shadows cast by the lime trees, life was going on in all its noisy variety. In spite of her resolution, she craved the chance to escape the shadow of Etienne's claustrophobic care. She needed to strike out on her own, if only for an hour or two.

The contrast between the air-conditioned comfort indoors and the oven of Malotte in late summer gave her quite a shock. Straight away, she realised that walking anywhere in this heat would make quite a statement. For the first few hundred metres, everything was fine. Then she left the town behind. Without the shadows cast by the buildings of Malotte, the feeling of heat increased. The road out of town was barren and dusty, making her journey more and more of a trial. The red-hot road reflected heat up into her face in a way the *maquis* would not, so she quickly abandoned the highway for a short cut across country. A sheep track ran diagonally up the slope towards the chateau. She suddenly knew where she was heading. She needed to be somewhere outside Etienne's influence—to escape, just for a short while. Trying to ignore the crippling heat, she headed towards the *gite*.

It looked dusty and deserted. It was nowhere near the luxury and comfort of Etienne's chateau, and yet the small bedroom, with all its lack of glamour, was one of the most wonderful things she'd seen for days. Exhausted, emotionally and physically drained, Gwen walked over to the bed and lay down in the wonderful, solitary silence.

She opened her eyes to find them filled with Etienne. 'What have you done to my baby?' he roared.

Gwen put a hand to her temple. 'Stop shouting… what on earth are you talking about?'

Dragging herself into a sitting position, her head full of cotton wool, she had the feeling his words wouldn't have made much more sense if she had been wide awake.

'I've been searching everywhere! Where have you been?'

He was furious. When she realised how the shadows had crept out of the corners of her bedroom, she knew why. She'd been sleeping for hours.

'Here, of course.'

That obviously wasn't the right answer. Etienne threw himself away from her bed and started pacing. Finally shaking herself free from sleep, Gwen shuffled her thoughts into order. 'And at the beautician's. That's all.'

Etienne was beside himself. He strode backwards and forwards, waving his arms in wordless fury.

'You never called a car!' he managed eventually. 'So I visited the salon to give you a lift myself. They said you'd left hours before. I tried Le Rossignol. They hadn't seen you. For all I knew, that meant you were trying to get back to Wales. You might have had an accident, or been picked up, or murdered, or worse... What were you thinking of? Why didn't you ring and tell me what you were doing? I drove up and down that road! Gwen, I've been—!' He lifted his arms into the air again, but the words wouldn't come. He let them drop with a bang.

Gwen looked at him in shock. She had never seen him like this. She hadn't been gone for long enough to deserve this level of anger, surely? Pushed beyond endurance, she opened her mouth to tell him what an arrogant, controlling, unbearable man he was when something in his eyes—some emotion quickly masked—stopped her. Suddenly, she remembered his first question.

'Hang on—*what* did you say about the baby, Etienne?' she asked abruptly.

Etienne's face froze. He seemed to be battling with himself. When he finally spoke, his voice was a whisper.

'Are you still pregnant?'

'Of course I am. You're not making sense. What are you talking about?'

'I was told you'd gone home. I assumed that meant Wales. You wanted to work, you didn't want to be a mother.' His voice was a crackle of fury. 'I thought you'd gone off to have an abortion.'

The word hit her like a slap in the face. Slowly, the real reason for his anger and the state of his appearance filtered through to her.

He was scared.

The only difference between them was that Etienne hadn't spent the last two days putting his fear into words. He had been trying to support her.

'No,' she said quietly. 'No, I'd never do that—especially not without telling you. How could you think such a thing?'

His hands were working, clenching and unclenching at his sides. She could tell he was building up to something terrible, long before he was able to put it into words.

'Because,' he said at last, and then had to draw in a ragged breath before continuing. 'Because of Angela.'

CHAPTER TEN

WITH those few words, Etienne pushed the final piece of jigsaw into place. Gwen remembered what she had read. She knelt up on the bed, facing him.

'Etienne,' she said carefully, 'please tell me the truth. What happened with her?'

He stared at her for a long, long time. Gwen stared back. She watched him work through more emotions than he could possibly name. Then suddenly, she saw him come to a decision. Whirling around, he strode towards the door.

Gwen got there just before he did. She could hardly hope to contain him. As she put a hand on either side of the doorframe she fully expected him to lift her straight out of his way. Instead he stopped. This time he refused to look at her.

'I can't talk about it.'

The coldness in his voice would have been enough of a warning for any other woman. Gwen stood her ground.

'I don't want to talk about it either—but we must.'

His silence spoke to her as loudly as the taut immobility of his body. It was obvious he did not know where to start. It was left to her to walk forward, her steps slow and hesitant. Every moment she expected him to turn away. He didn't. When she was as close as she could get, she put her hand up to his face. Still he did not move. With the pad of her thumb she stroked away the crease between his dark brows. As she did so, she felt the brush of his thick dark lashes against her palm. He had closed his eyes. Then he nodded.

Gwen took the initiative. 'I was telling the truth, Etienne. I really didn't know anything about your association with Angela before you mentioned her name. That led me to the Internet, but it was hard to recognise you from the reports I read. Your reaction to—' she looked down at her waist awkwardly, unwilling to put it into words '—well, all *this* was so different from what I expected, given what was supposed to have happened back then. I don't know what to think,' she said softly.

'I would never want to get rid of a baby,' he announced. 'Then, or now.'

That explained a lot. Gwen's sympathy for Angela Webbington began to waver. There was indeed more to this story than she had been able to uncover before she lost her nerve.

'All my life I had everything, except a real family. My father merely did his duty in providing a Malotte heir. That was the extent of it,' Etienne began with difficulty. He was tracking back over an unbearably painful time and considering each word. 'I knew there had to be more to life than that. I searched far and wide for something to fill that emptiness. Angela was beautiful, successful, and totally unlike anything the House of

Malotte had seen in its entire history. When I got engaged to her, I assumed we would have the perfect partnership. I was wrong. That one error of judgement still haunts me. Angela wanted the Moreau lifestyle, but none of its responsibilities. She could spend and party as hard as I could, but it was beyond her to be faithful. She was neither loyal, nor even honest. Our relationship soon hit the rocks. Finally, she went behind my back and terminated that pregnancy before bothering to inform me she was carrying a child. She called the baby "a body-wrecking disruption to my career".' He stopped as his voice twisted with emotion.

Gwen couldn't begin to imagine what living through that showdown must have felt like. Nothing she could say would ease his pain, so she kept quiet.

'I had always given her a totally free rein,' he continued. 'She did what she liked, and never stopped to think about me or the baby. At the end, she taunted me that she couldn't be sure the baby was even mine. When I found out you were—' He stopped and opened his eyes, clearly wondering what her reaction would be if he said the word.

'*Pregnant*.' She supplied it for him. 'It's OK. I can take it now.'

'I was so determined the same thing was not going to happen again,' he continued grimly. 'I wanted things done properly this time, right from the beginning. Yet that has turned out to be wrong, too.'

'Yes, it has!' Gwen burst out. She couldn't keep quiet any longer. 'You've been heavy-handed, but I should have thought about you as well as myself—should have realised something was wrong. But now we know more about what has pulled us apart, we can work at getting back together. Can't we?' She looked searchingly into his face.

Etienne's expression was guarded.

'That's up to you,' he said at length.

It was a start.

'OK,' Gwen said slowly, feeling her way towards a conversation they should have had long ago. 'Get the doctor back in, and I'll promise to listen to his advice this time, as long as he's a little nicer to me and minds his manners!' She smiled softly and then went on. 'Pregnancy has been the biggest shock of my life—you can't imagine what it's been like. But I'm getting used to it,' she said, still trying to convince herself. 'And I'm going to take the greatest care of our baby, believe me. But in return, I need something to do. I can't sit around all day, being waited on hand, foot and finger. It will drive me mad, Etienne!'

He put a hand tentatively on her shoulder. 'If I let you go back to Le Rossignol, you'll overdo it.'

'Of course I won't!' she scoffed, sliding her arms around his waist and giving him a reassuring squeeze. They both knew taking it easy would be a struggle for her. There was another long, uncomfortable silence.

'Perhaps I could prove it to you,' she offered eventually. 'If you came to work with me, you could enjoy yourself in the restaurant while I'm fiddling about in my kitchens. You'll be on hand to make sure I don't lift anything heavier than a paring knife, and I'll have one eye on you, watching for the first signs of boredom. You can be the one who says when it's time to go home. I might even let you drive me, in my car!' She threw his old insolence back at him archly. 'But only when I get too big to fit behind the wheel.'

Etienne looked down at her with a sudden spark. 'You called the chateau "home"!'

Gwen looked equally startled. 'I did, didn't I? Am I allowed to do that?' She tried to coax a smile from him. 'Do you mind?'

'Of course I don't,' he whispered into the fragrant silk of her hair. 'I went overboard in trying to do the right thing, but it was only when I thought I'd lost you that I realised why. It isn't only the baby, Gwen. I want you, pure and simple—you, and our own family, and our real, living home.'

'That's what I want, too,' she said. 'If only we had both realised from the start what that word meant, it would have saved us all this heartache.'

She had felt so helpless in the face of Etienne's relentless efficiency. Now she saw she had been deaf and blind to his feelings, too.

He looked into her eyes. His expression was filled with such uncomplicated emotion that she held her breath.

'Gwen, I thought Angela had killed all the human parts of me. Then you came along, and showed me how to live again. I never imagined you would leave me. When you seemed to walk out of my life, I realised that love is like sand. The harder you try and hold onto it, the faster it slips away between your fingers.'

Gwen knew this was as close as he would come to opening his heart to her. His skin felt warm and firm beneath her fingers. She felt his soft breath stir her hair.

It tickled, but nothing would have tempted her to move. For long, wonderful moments she relaxed against him. They were together again, and she was in his arms. That was all she cared about. And then something he had said filtered back through the misty happiness filling her mind.

'Love?' she repeated. 'Etienne…?' She paused—unable to summon the courage to finish the sentence.

He stirred. She felt it through the creased, damp ruin of his designer shirt. When he spoke, she realised it was the movement of a restless spirit trying to settle.

'That depends on you.' He spoke with an alien hesitancy. She laid her head against his chest again, and listened to the familiar sound of his heart beating. It had lost the hectic rhythm of a few moments before, and now her own pulse quickened.

With her face safely hidden from him, Gwen allowed herself a small smile. 'No, it doesn't. I was a victim of my heart the first moment I saw you, Etienne. I didn't know it then, but one look at you across that crowded restaurant and I was lost. You came and found me, and that was it. Although I never thought you could feel for me in the way I feel for you now.'

When she said that his arms tightened around her, but he said nothing. She smiled and closed her eyes. Silently, he was giving her all the reassurance she needed.

'My body took control that night. To become anything more than your mistress was a hopeless dream. I realised that. It was why I had to end things. We were opposites in everything.'

'Well, they do say opposites attract,' he said quietly.

Gwen nuzzled against him. She was so happy words

were barely necessary but Etienne had exposed his soul to her. It only made her love him more, and she wanted to make the next time easier for him.

'Could we begin all over again?' she said softly. 'Can we start looking forward as a couple now?'

In answer, he bent and kissed her. He did it so reverently she could hardly believe he was the same vigorous lover who had blazed through her life like a comet. She melted against him. Her response fired him with all the passion that had waited so long to be released.

'Does this reaction mean there's one part of our past you might still want to remember?' he murmured huskily into her neck. At the touch of his lips, Gwen quivered and went limp in his arms.

'That was an incredible night, Etienne,' she breathed.

He was holding her captive against his hard, hot body. She had dreamed of this moment for so long. Now it was here, she could not wait.

'I need you, Etienne…' Her voice was a long, slow gasp of desire.

'How much?' he growled. 'As much as when I gave you our baby?'

'More,' she moaned. 'More…'

His hand moved to cradle her ripening breast. As his thumb described slow, thoughtful circles over her nipple it reacted by swelling to a full peak.

'Your body delights me more and more each day,' he murmured into her ear. Then without another word he lifted her up and carried her back to the bed. Sculpting pillows into soft shapes beneath her tender body, he lay down beside her. His eyes were soft, but his voice was hoarse with anticipation. 'I've missed you so much, Gwen.'

She chuckled. 'If you've missed anyone, it's that girl in four-inch heels and the beautiful dress. Not Our Gwen from the valley with her morning sickness and a desperate need to get back to work.'

'You're wrong. Knowing that you're far too stubborn to change is one of the many things I love about you. One of the things that makes you so special.' He silenced her with another kiss, this time as light as thistledown. 'And now...I want to see you naked again. It has been such a long, lonely time for both of us. Let me look at you.'

Without a word he undid her blouse, one button at a time. His movements were slow and considered. Anticipation rose up in her like a fountain. Flicking the sides of her shirt apart, he looked down with pride at the taut white lace of her bra. With movements so slow they made Gwen want to scream with urgency, he slid his hands beneath her arching body and unclipped the strap. Lifting the bra up, he exposed her breasts. Both showed the delicate tracery of pressure marks where their increasing size had been compressed.

'Oh, poor baby,' he murmured, and Gwen knew he wasn't speaking to the tiny creature growing inside her. Lowering his head, he started by laying a gentle network of kisses over each breast in turn. Then, as the warm fragrance of her femininity aroused him, his foreplay quickened. His fingers were greedy for the experience of her body. His skill made her writhe beneath him. As he towered over her she prepared for the onslaught her body craved but Etienne had other ideas. He rolled over onto his back.

'You do it. You're in charge.' His words were ragged with desire. 'I don't want to hurt either of you.'

'I won't let you,' Gwen whispered, sliding over his body until they connected with a mutual moan of pleasure.

Etienne's delight in Gwen's body increased her hunger for him. Their lovemaking excited her beyond the point of distraction. She forgot everything except what he meant to her. It was only hours later, when she woke in his bed at the chateau, that it all came flooding back on a tide of morning sickness.

Etienne sat up the moment he felt her stir. Instantly, he hit the remote control to pull the curtains right back from his tall windows.

'Is that enough light for you to reach the bathroom?'

Nodding, Gwen made a bolt for anonymity. His cool and luxurious wet room was a perfect sanctuary. When she felt better, she had a shower and washed her hair. Emerging refreshed, she revelled in the sight of Etienne gazing at her like a connoisseur admiring his latest treasure. There was something about being desired when she felt so unlovable that warmed Gwen's soul. Hot summer sunshine pouring through his windows thawed her still further. Padding back to his big, wide bed, she stretched out across it like a cat.

Etienne smiled as though he were the one who had been at the cream. 'Flaunt yourself like that, Miss Williams, and I shall make you *very* late for work,' he drawled.

'Good,' Gwen said smartly.

'You're humouring me.' He chuckled. 'From now on, I'm never going to forget what Le Rossignol means to you.'

She reached out, trailing a finger around the outline of the face she loved so much. 'Myself, I'm beginning to wonder. You've opened my eyes, Etienne. While I was working all hours, I kept telling myself it was the most important thing in my life. It was only when I realised what you'd been through that I began to get things into perspective. I was kidding myself. You are the only thing I truly can't live without. But I still don't know how I'm going to cope with a family of our own—'

'We're a team, Gwen,' he said hoarsely. 'I want to make things better for you, but I don't always know how.' As he spoke he gathered her up, wet hair, damp towels and all.

'Talk to me. Tell me things, Etienne. Give me something to think about outside of work, and I'll do the same for you. Up until now I've sacrificed my social life and worked extra hard, because I thought no one could love me as much as my family did. Then I found you, but it went wrong and I missed out on all the romance of a proposal. You took control, and that was that. I wanted to be wooed and won, not organised out of existence. That was why I needed that break after my spell at the beautician's!'

With a gasp of relief, Etienne seized on her words and pulled himself onto firmer ground. 'You want romance, *mon amour*? I can at least manage that, in one small way.' Slipping from her arms, he went to find his jacket. It was on the floor, where he had dropped it the night before in the throes of passion. Rifling through his pockets, he pulled out a small leather box and returned to the bedside.

'You appeared in my life like a dream, Gwen, and I want to keep that feeling alive,' he whispered softly. 'That's why I want to give you this. It's a family heirloom. I was going to present it to you at the exact moment our baby is born. That's why I've been carrying it everywhere, in my pocket. But I think it would be much better to give it to you now…'

'What is it?' she probed, like a surgeon looking for trouble.

He raised one eyebrow, mocking her gently. 'I'm going to make at least one of your dreams come true right now.'

Before Gwen knew what was happening, he went down on one knee in front of her. Then he held out the little box.

'Would you do me the honour of becoming my wife, Gwen?'

'But, Etienne…you've already decided that's going to happen…' she said, teasingly.

'I know, and that was wrong of me. I want us to start again, too. This is my proposal. When you accept—'

'*When?*' She laughed, ruffling his hair playfully. 'You still sound very sure of yourself!'

'*If* you accept,' he corrected himself gravely, 'then I shall sweep you off to Wales, where you can have such a big church wedding and lavish reception that it will be talked about for years to come. Then we'll have a honeymoon. When and where is entirely up to you. I want it to be this instant, but when it comes to our life together, Gwen, I've issued my last direct order.'

She was floating on a cloud of disbelief. 'Are you sure? After all, ordering people about is what you do.'

He had a swift answer for that. 'And so do you, when you're at work. That was part of the problem. I underestimated how much you enjoy being in control.'

She smiled. 'I moved away from my family to get a taste of independence. Once I had it, I didn't want to let go. That's why I was so unhappy. You changed so much once we found out I was pregnant.'

'That's why I want you to feel we're together because it's what we *both* want, Gwen. Now I know what makes you so independent, I can allow for that. We may have got things out of sequence but this can be our second chance. What do you say?'

She put her slender, pale hands over his wide brown ones and drew him to his feet.

'I can't think of anything I would like more than to be your wife, Etienne.'

She wanted to say a lot more, but he was in no mood to listen. Pulling her into his arms, he kissed her until she was breathless and laughing with delight.

'Then you'll need this.'

Taking a stunning diamond solitaire from the little ring box, he placed it gently on her finger. With a gasp, Gwen watched it split the sunlight into a rainbow of colours. Then she looked at him with eyes full of longing.

'This ring is absolutely wonderful, Etienne, but all I *really* need is you!'

millsandboon.co.uk Community

Join Us!

The Community is the perfect place to meet and chat to kindred spirits who love books and reading as much as you do, but it's also the place to:

- **Get the inside scoop from authors about their latest books**
- **Learn how to write a romance book with advice from our editors**
- **Help us to continue publishing the best in women's fiction**
- **Share your thoughts on the books we publish**
- **Befriend other users**

Forums: Interact with each other as well as authors, editors and a whole host of other users worldwide.

Blogs: Every registered community member has their own blog to tell the world what they're up to and what's on their mind.

Book Challenge: We're aiming to read 5,000 books and have joined forces with The Reading Agency in our inaugural Book Challenge.

Profile Page: Showcase yourself and keep a record of your recent community activity.

Social Networking: We've added buttons at the end of every post to share via digg, Facebook, Google, Yahoo, technorati and de.licio.us.

www.millsandboon.co.uk

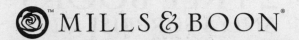

2 FREE BOOKS
AND A SURPRISE GIFT

We would like to take this opportunity to thank you for reading this Mills & Boon® book by offering you the chance to take TWO more specially selected books from the Modern™ series absolutely FREE! We're also making this offer to introduce you to the benefits of the Mills & Boon® Book Club™—

- **FREE home delivery**
- **FREE gifts and competitions**
- **FREE monthly Newsletter**
- **Exclusive Mills & Boon Book Club offers**
- **Books available before they're in the shops**

Accepting these FREE books and gift places you under no obligation to buy, you may cancel at any time, even after receiving your free books. Simply complete your details below and return the entire page to the address below. You don't even need a stamp!

YES Please send me 2 free Modern books and a surprise gift. I understand that unless you hear from me, I will receive 4 superb new books every month for just £3.19 each, postage and packing free. I am under no obligation to purchase any books and may cancel my subscription at any time. The free books and gift will be mine to keep in any case.

Ms/Mrs/Miss/Mr _____ Initials _____

Surname _____

Address _____

_____ Postcode _____

E-mail _____

Send this whole page to: Mills & Boon Book Club, Free Book Offer, FREEPOST NAT 10298, Richmond, TW9 1BR